MW01537512

Half A Life

A Novel by

Christopher Louis

This book is a work of fiction. Any resemblance to places, people, or events is completely coincidental.

Visit
Christopher Louis
www.christopherlouisauthor.com

To my partner Stacey. You have been my rock through so much. I love you more than words can adequately express.

Dedicated to the memory of my beloved mother Pamela.

PART ONE

Benjamin

"Uhh . . ."

Ben woke with startled ecstasy as he felt the pulsing of his stomach and groin going into hype drive. It took him a moment to awaken enough to fully realize what had happened. He reached under the blanket and felt the front of his underwear; it was hot, wet and sticky.

"Damn." He cursed. This was the third time this week that his libido had taken over with the same results. He couldn't help but recall the talk his father had given him about not being scared if he woke up to find white sticky stuff in his underpants. He had tried to tell his father he already knew about ejaculation but his father insisted he hear it from him so Ben would know the facts. At the time Ben had never imagined it happening to him, but here it was for the third time.

Pushing the blankets off he silently slid out of bed and shuffled to the dresser to get a clean pair of underwear. With the new pair in his hands he made his way to the door, carefully opened it then tip-toed to the bathroom. He didn't want to wake anyone. The last thing he needed was for his little brother Ryan coming in asking him what he was doing. Ryan was too young to know what a wet dream was; he'd have to sit through the talk with their father soon enough. Ben stripped the soiled pair off and gave them a quick rinse in the sink before dropping them into the hamper. He pulled the new pair on and tip-toed back to his room.

He pulled the blankets tighter around himself and recalled what he'd been dreaming about. It had been another locker room dream and once again it had David playing a prominent role. He didn't understand it; three dreams all including his best friend. Tonight's dream had obviously taken the sexual route as his others had, but it was nothing compared to two nights ago; in that dream he and David were archaeologists exploring the chambers of a newly discovered pyramid. He guessed the dream took the direction it did as they had been studying Ancient Egypt in History class for the past couple of weeks.

The dream started with them walking through a tunnel attempting to read and decipher the hieroglyphics that lined the walls. David stopped to examine a particularly difficult section when Ben tripped and stumbled into a false wall that opened up to a hidden burial chamber. As they examined their find they discovered the tomb was a double chamber for a Pharaoh and his male lover. Reading the hieroglyphs they learned that the lover had died of natural causes and the king took his own life weeks later; he claimed to be unable to go on without the other.

The dream shifted to Ben and David at their campsite going over their findings, cataloging the tomb's contents. David was talking about the king and his lover and said that he would do the same if something ever happened to Ben. The dream shifted again and the two were now naked and making love. Ben woke just as the dream reached it most intense moment. It had been the most powerful dream he had ever had. At the time he didn't think anything of the fact that David had been the object of his desire, but now he started questioning why.

Ben had spent a great deal of time recently trying to figure out why he felt so different. As his friends were talking about sex or girls, he'd find himself feeling almost isolated; he just didn't share their feelings or thoughts. He didn't pay it much thought at first, he had been on dates and was still a popular guy. Sure when he dated someone more than a couple a times the mere mention of sex brought his brain to a halt but he assumed that was normal. He wasn't ready for sex yet, he wanted something more than a quick fix and whenever he explained that the girls always seemed to understand. Whenever his friends at school pressed him about his escapades he had always been able to just shrug and say it was none of their business. He was popular enough for it not to be a problem. Plus his history of past girlfriends, Karen in particular, was enough for his friends to understand why.

It wasn't until about two months ago that he finally realized that his reluctance, as well as his almost non-existent desire, was due to the fact that he wasn't sexually attracted to girls; boys, however, were a totally different matter. The realization that every time he masturbated it was a boy he was thinking about freaked him out at first. The more he tried to stop, the stronger his desires came. There was no denying it; the pieces feel into place. He felt like blinders had been removed from his eyes; everything made sense at last.

Discovering and accepting that he was gay brought a hunger to Ben that he hadn't had before. He wanted to know anything and everything he could. He'd spend hours surfing the net for anything he could find about gay teens. He was writing in his journal and sharing his thoughts but even that wasn't feeding his hunger. During his weekly homework visit to the library he would leave David and Sarah at their usual table to hunt out obscure titles or articles. Knowing what an avid reader Ben was, his friends didn't seem to notice. The hardest part was checking the items out without them seeing what they were. He'd even begun going on nights where David or Sarah had to work so he didn't have to hide anything.

In the past couple of weeks Ben read more books than he had in years. He was pleased to find some great novels and stories; his favorite being the ones that had characters close in age to himself. Last week, he finally got up the nerve to go to the Gay and Lesbian bookstore downtown. He learned about the store on his first night of surfing the net but had been too scared to go. The moment he entered he felt a sense of welcome envelop him; the images of two men or two women holding hands and/or kissing made him giddy.

After what seemed an eternity of him simply standing in the entrance looking around in awe a young woman with short cropped hair and a dozen earrings approached, welcomed him, and asked if he needed some help. His awe disappeared and he instantly started babbling about recently discovering his sexuality and that he was looking for novels. The clerk (Donna, he'd learn later) led him to a series of shelves and a deep conversation commenced about the books he'd already read and what drew him to those titles. Had he not been limited with the amount of money he had on him he would have bought more than just the three books he did. He thanked the clerk for her help and rushed home. That night he holed himself up in his room devouring each book. Had Sarah not phoned at her normal time he would have probably read all night.

He experienced his first dream that night. The one constant in each of the dreams was that David had been the object of his desire. At first he assumed it was because he and David were so close; they'd been inseparable since second grade. Was it possible that his feelings for David were becoming something more than just friendship? He did have to admit that David was cute; the way his brown hair was always slightly messy in that adorable way or the way his green eyes always seemed to shine when he laughed or told a joke. He knew that David was the envy of many of their other friends with his v-shaped frame and strong arms; plus he did have that amazing bubble butt.

"Oh shit! I just thought of my friend's butt as amazing." Ben whispered. As the realization came, he noticed that he was getting another erection. It was true; he was turned on by his best friend.

His first impulse was to pick up his cell and call Sarah, but it was the middle of the night for starters and second he wondered if he could truly tell her about this. He and Sarah had been friends since they were four years old and always shared everything with each other, but this . . . this was different. Even when he'd been sneaking around the library he always thought he would tell Sarah and David eventually; when the time was right. Now however, his plans for how events were going to play out hit a snag. Besides he knew he'd have to do it in person, if and when he did. This was far too big for a phone call. He knew she would be okay with the gay part, thanks to her boyfriend Christian; Sarah was one of the most diversely accepting people he knew. However, his having feelings for David, that was a whole other issue.

Ben pushed the what-ifs from his mind. If not he'd never get back to sleep. He yawned and pulled the blankets up to his chin, closed his eyes and let sleep return. He drifted into slumber with visions of David and him dancing in his head.

David

David woke instantly at the sound of a door slamming shut. He held his breathe as he waited for the footsteps to come; sure enough they came but they weren't the heavy menacing stomps of his drunken father, but the soft click of his mother's slippers. Like his father's usually did, they stopped outside his door; he glanced over his pillow and saw the shadow under the door. His mother seemed to be facing his door but wasn't coming in; after a moment she moved away and he heard the bathroom door open.

David finally allowed himself a chance to breathe audibly. His heart was beating so fast it was knocking his chest and he was sure his father could have heard it. This had been the fourth time tonight he'd been jarred awake by his parents. The clock read 3:43 am, the latest they had ever woken him before. He didn't know how he could handle a beating this late and manage to face school in a couple of hours. Just one more day he thought and then he would be gone for the whole weekend with Ben and Sarah at the Tolliver's cabin. Three whole nights of sleep without waking to even the slightest sound; it was more than he could hope for.

David hadn't always been scared of his father. In fact he and his dad used to have a joyous father-son bond. The best was when they would talk about soccer while fixing up an old hot rod in the garage. They knew it would probably never run again but they didn't care. It was something they did together.

His dad had once been the proud father who always shouted the loudest at matches making sure everyone knew it was his son to make the latest goal. He was always in the front row at the band concerts or buying the most of whatever it was David would be selling for fund raising. He told everyone how proud he was of his son the soccer star and drummer.

That all changed last year; his dad had gone from proud parent to volatile drunk overnight, all due to him walking in on David masturbating. At first his father was calm and collected attempting to say how natural it was for a boy to be curious; however the calmness vanished when he noticed that it was a gay magazine David was masturbating to. His father became enraged; he rushed at his son and slapped his face. He yanked the magazine out of his hands, rolled it into a tube and began using it to beat David. David attempted to cover himself while at the same time attempting to keep from being hit but his father's rage was too strong.

David's mother rushed into the room and attempted to get her husband to stop but he continued his attack. His mother was finally able to get her husband to stop long enough to explain what was going on. His father threw the magazine in her face and told her to ask the little faggot. When she didn't do anything but toss the magazine to the side and hug David, his father started pacing and telling her that there was no way he was going to have an evil little heathen living under his roof. His father left the room and then left the house with shouts of "burning in hell" and "God will punish him".

His father never returned that night but eventually returned the following night; his decent into drunkenness began. Most days his father wouldn't come home until after 10 pm and always drunk. He'd avoid David at all cost, if he did happen to look at him he would only refer to him with a derogatory name, his favorite being faggot. A week after the drinking started, David was shaken awake by the sound of his bedroom door being kicked open. Before he could figure out what was happening his father was at his bed, he latched on to his hair and dragged him from the bed. He was kicked, punched and preached to until his father stumbled and lost his balance, which was quicker than David could have hoped for.

The attacks continued from that night forward; they happened about once a week but never on the same night. With his athletic background David could endure the beatings most times by blocking his father's drunken attacks, but it was the psychological abuse that hurt him the most. He never knew when they would happen; if it wasn't a beating, his father would march up and down the hallway preaching and yelling his disgust. He would stop outside David's door and bang throughout; every night he wondered if tonight was the night. His only saving grace was that his father usually quit by 1:00 am. Tonight however, it had been long after his normal quitting time. David prayed this wasn't a new form of torment.

He heard the toilet flush and his mother's quick walk past his room. When he heard his parent's door shut he heard some mumblings but he couldn't make them out. The door opened again and he knew this time it was his father. The loud staccato of his steps brought a cold sweat to David's face as his fear snapped to attention. He braced himself for the inevitable kick on the door; it didn't come. His father walked right past into the kitchen and out the back door. He heard his father's car start; he didn't relax until he was sure the car was out of the driveway and halfway down the street.

He said a silent prayer and lay back onto his pillow. He closed his eyes; he needed to get some sleep. Before he could even start to relax he heard his mother rushing towards his room. She knocked then opened the door.

"David? Honey, are you awake?"

"Yeah, what is it mom?"

She didn't say anything at first, she entered and walked straight to his closet and pulled out his suitcase. David sat up and wondered what she was doing.

"David, I need you to pack some things and head over to the Davidson's hotel. I've already called them and told them to expect you. I'll join you in the morning. But for now I need you to pack and leave."

"What? Mom, what are you talking about?"

She didn't stop to look at him. She hefted the suitcase onto the bed and hurried to the dresser and started opening drawers. David left the bed and touched his mother's arm. She didn't stop pulling clothes from the drawers.

"Mom?"

"We don't have much time David, your father will be back soon and I want you out of here."

"Where did dad go?"

His mother finally stopped and looked up at her son. David could see the panic in her eyes.

"I'm not sure." She paused as she seemed to struggle with to say. "Your father . . . your father said that you better not be here when he gets back or else."

The cold sweat returned instantly. He didn't want to ask or hear what she would say next, but before he could stop himself he asked the question.

"Why shouldn't I be here?"

His mother couldn't look at him. She stifled a cry and said. "He . . . he said . . . if you were here he'd kill you."

Benjamin

Ben spooned the last of his cereal into his mouth, dropped the bowl into the sink, swallowed, and danced along to the music blaring from the radio as he made his way to the foyer. His jacket and book bag were already waiting; his mom must have brought them down after making his bed. He liked how his mom seemed old fashioned in her ways of doing things like making the beds, having his jacket ready or making his lunch; complete with a fruit and a vegetable. At the same time she was very down to earth and willing to let Ben have some freedom. Not many of his friends were allowed to set their own curfews or have rock music blaring through the house at 7:00 am.

He double checked his hair in the hall mirror, adjusted a few strands and then gave up. He pulled on his jacket and nudged the off button on the radio with his foot. He pulled the curtain from the window, checking for Sarah; no sign of her yet. He wanted this day over; he couldn't wait to get out of the city. He wanted to spend the weekend at his favorite place in the world -the cabin; especially since David and Sarah would be joining them for the trip. It wasn't often that the three of them all got to skip out of one day of school. Usually when David and Sarah joined them for a trip to the cabin, it was for a weekend or overnight trip. Sometimes they'd even go over school breaks. He had been so happy when his parents first suggested that since they were going away for this business meeting that Ben invite his friends. It had been touch and go for a moment with David's parents, but finally they relented and agreed he could miss one day of school. The trips to the cabin were made all the more better with Sarah and David.

He heard Sarah's car pull into the driveway.

"I'm off mom! I'll see you this afternoon."

"Bye sweetie. Have a good day!" She announced from upstairs.

He grabbed his bag and ran out the front door. It was much colder than he thought; the shining sun was quite deceiving. He pulled his collar tighter around his neck. He had been sick of the cold and snow and hoped it would start to warm up soon, but no such luck today. He ducked into the car, pleased to find it warm.

"Come on, we've got to go."

"What's the hurry; it's like ten minutes to school. We've got at least twenty." He said as he buckled his seat belt. He was about to turn on the radio but stopped when he saw the serious look on Sarah's face.

"What's up?" He asked but she didn't answer right away. "Did something happen? Did you and Christian have a fight?" He joked hoping that bringing up the boyfriend would put a smile on her face. It had no effect.

"No."

Wow, no smile for the mention of Christian; he knew it was serious. Her brow tightened as she drove and he noticed that she was playing with the end of her pony tail. Before he could ask again, she swung the car into the drive-thru of a fast food restaurant and ordered them each a coffee. Okay, Ben thought, this is weird; Sarah never drank coffee unless she was tired or sick. He examined her closer and noticed that she wasn't wearing any make-up and that her blond hair wasn't as shiny as usual. Her eyes were bloodshot and her cheeks looked flush.

"Sarah, what the hell is going on?"

Retrieving their coffees, she pulled the car back onto the road but didn't take the road leading to school.

"We're going to the hotel."

Sarah's parents owned and operated an old hotel that during the 20's and 30's had been one of the most glamorous hotels in the state. However during the next couple of decades its ownership changed hands so many times that the hotel had fallen into disrepair. When her parents bought the hotel in the 80's (dirt cheap Sarah always liked to joke) they had taken it upon themselves to transform it back to a place of grandeur. Ben loved to spend time there; it was almost like the cabin, a place to escape to. He, David and Sarah spent so much time there that Sarah's parents set aside a room for David and him in the family wing.

"Why?" As much as he loved to go there before, he was

apprehensive now. Something was wrong, something he didn't know.

"It's . . . its David." Sarah finally announced after a lengthy silence.

"Is he alright? Did . . . what . . . what happened?"

Fear took hold of Ben. What could have happened to David? Was he safe? Was he okay? Did something happen with his parents? He could only guess, but assumed something happened with his father. Mr. Whitman had changed so drastically in the past year; he stopped coming to games or concerts and whenever he or Sarah called the house he'd hang up on them. David never talked about it, he just shrugged it off. The most he would say was his dad was drinking heavily.

"David arrived at the hotel about 4:30 this morning."

"What? Why?"

Sarah shrugged. "I wish I had more to tell you Ben, but I don't. Mom woke me up and told me that David's mom called her. She said Mrs. Whitman was frantic and begged mom to let David come and stay with us. I got dressed and we waited for him to arrive. When he did, I took him to your room; he didn't say much. He looked dazed. All he said is he couldn't talk then. He asked if he could have some time alone and that he would explain later to both you and me."

"Um . . . oh . . ." Ben didn't know what else to say.

"Yeah." Sarah sighed.

The remainder of the drive was silent; neither of them could think of anything else to say. When they arrived at the hotel Sarah parked the car but neither moved. They were both anxious to see their friend but also nervous. They met each others glances and with a nod of encouragement they entered the lobby and slowly climbed the steps to the family wing.

They stood outside the door for a moment, they were so used to coming and going without knocking but now it didn't seem right. Ben raised his hand, paused a moment and then rapped quickly. They didn't hear anything for a moment, but then they heard the David's faint reply of "Come in."

Ben wasn't sure what to expect when he opened the door but it certainly wasn't David sitting on the floor at the end of one of the beds staring at his clenched hands. David appeared okay, his hair was messier than normal and he was wearing pajama pants and a sweatshirt; Ben knew this was how he had arrived this morning. It was hard to see their friend so silent and unlike himself. He was the joker of the group. He was always finding something to laugh about. Now, however, he looked lost. It was a complete contrast to the young boy who had won Ben and Sarah over with his boisterous laughter so many years ago.

Ben and Sarah joined David on the floor, each sitting on either side of him.

"David?" Sarah was the first to speak.

He didn't respond verbally; he nodded his head a few times and forced a smile. Ben knew it was his way of trying to show them he was okay.

"Life . . ." David finally spoke. "Life really sucks sometimes." He started to laugh but stopped before it turned to tears.

Ben was about to ask a question but Sarah beat him to it.

"What happened?"

"My father . . . my father, the man I once admired so much." He took a deep breathe. "He hates me. He hates me."

"What?" Sarah asked.

David held himself so tightly; Ben could tell that he was trying to keep from crying.

"He hates me Sarah. For the last year he hasn't once called me by my name. Its always asshole, shit-head, dick-face or . . . or . . . fa . . . it doesn't matter." He held back a sob. "He won't say anything to me. Then . . . then there are the fights and the punches."

He couldn't hold it in any longer; his body rocked with his deep sobs. Both Sarah and Ben quickly wrapped their arms around him as the tears flew not only from David but from both of them as well.

"David?" Ben said once the tears and sobs slowed. "How did this happen? I mean what . . . how . . .?" He wasn't sure how to finish his own question; nothing seemed appropriate.

David rubbed the tears from his cheeks and his eyes as finally looked at Ben. Ben braced himself for the moment of truth.

"Last year my dad came into my room and he . . . he . . . he caught me . . . you know . . ." He cleared his throat and forced a nervous laugh. "You know . . . whacking. Um . . . well he just went berserk and started yelling and hitting me. He told me I was a disgusting pervert who was disrespecting him and God."

Ben and Sarah shared looks of disbelief. David nodded knowingly and continued.

"He ignored me for the next couple of nights but then he started preaching about how I was going to hell. I thought for sure it would pass and that he'd get over it . . . but . . ." He wiped tears away again. "I was wrong. He continued hitting me; most times . . . most times I could defend myself but, but there were times he was simply too strong."

Sarah placed a gentle hand on David's cheek. "Why didn't you tell us?"

"I . . . I couldn't. He would have done . . . done something worst to me."

"But David if we would have known, maybe we could have . . . um . . ."

David sniffled. "What could you have done?"

"We would have helped." Ben added now. He tried to sound confident and strong, though he knew he wouldn't have known what to do.

"We would have done anything to help you!" Sarah added quickly, her bravado replacing her tears. "We would have kicked his ass!"

The group each managed smiles and brief laughs. They shared a group hug before they broke apart and returned to their original positions.

"What happened last night?" Ben said after a few moments of silence.

"He . . ." David took another deep breathe. "He told my mom that I better not be there when he got home or he'd . . . he'd kill me."

Ben felt as if he'd been sucker-punched. It was difficult to breathe. How could anyone say they were going to kill their own son? It was inconceivable. Never in his life could he ever imagine that his own parents would ever feel such a way. He couldn't believe that David had been able to hide this for so long.

"My father . . . he was going to kill me. He was going to kill me. Kill me . . . kill me . . ."

"Stop, David! Please stop saying that." Ben pleaded. He couldn't stand hearing those words.

David pulled himself from his friends and started to pace the floor. "I . . . I need . . . I need some air." He paused and looked at his friends. "Can we get out of here?"

"Absolutely!" The both voiced in unison. There had been no need to answer though; they would go or do whatever David needed them to.

Benjamin

The group bundled up in their coats, hats and scarves then began a trek through the trails behind the hotel. The further they walked the more animated David became. The bite of the wind on his cheeks and the crunch of his boots in the snow seemed to revive him. He talked and joked as if their conversation of a few minutes ago was nothing. Ben wasn't fooled though; he could see the pain lingering in his eyes.

They let David lead them through their favorite trail which led to the lake. It wasn't a private lake by any means but as long as they had been coming here it was always empty so they called it theirs. During the summer they would spend hours sitting with their feet in the water, talking and hanging out. Some times they would even trek out here at night and have bonfires.

The water was still but the trickling sounds of water were still present. They each sat upon the fallen tree trunk nearest the edge and let the serenity envelope them; David closed his eyes, and Sarah drew hearts in the snow with a stick. Ben contemplated his life; his own personal issues paled in comparison to David's problems. He couldn't imagine what his friend had been going through. He'd been suffering so much lately and yet somehow managed to hide it from them despite the fact that they saw each other almost everyday either through school or practice; then there were the constant emails, texts, chats, and phone calls.

Wait a moment Ben thought, he began to recall seeing a couple of bruises on David a few times in the locker room. He'd always assumed they'd come from practice, but now he knew that wasn't the case. The more he thought about it the more he realized the bruises were in places he wouldn't normally associate from soccer. Why hadn't he thought them odd before? David wasn't clumsy or prone to getting hit with the ball; he was one of the best players on the team. If only he had put two and two together earlier he might have been able to help his friend. But that brought him right back to where they were a while ago; what could he or Sarah truly have done? All he could do now was be here for David; lend him a shoulder or hand. David and Sarah were his dearest friends and he loved them both; even with his other feelings surfacing recently, he would stand by his friend and help in any way he could.

"Thank you both, for listening. I . . . I don't know what I would do without you." David said breaking the comfortable silence that had encompassed them.

"You're the third musketeer; "all for one and one for all" and all that other shit. You're stuck with us!" Sarah said with gusto. They had always hated the musketeer reference; it had started in fourth grade when they had played the characters in a skit and it stuck with them ever since;

today it brought smiles and laughter to each of them.

"Thanks!" David said in fake annoyance. "So . . . is it just me or your assess freezing too?"

"Oh God yes!" Sarah jumped from the stump rubbing her hands over her butt in an attempt to warm it.

"I was wondering if it was just me." Ben added.

"Race you back."

Sarah bolted from the scene heading back through the trails. Ben and David shared a look of annoyance; they shrugged and quickly joined in the race.

David

Their run continued to the hotel entrance. Had circumstances been different they would have raced inside and up the stairs into Sarah's room where they would drop to floor laughing. However that wasn't the case today; they waited outside until they caught their breath. David noticed his mother's car as well as Ben's parent's SVU in the parking lot. He pointed them out to the others and saw the same questioning looks on their faces; they knew David's mom would be coming but were unsure why Ben's parents were there.

The trio entered the hotel and found all their parents waiting for them. Mrs. Whitman was the first to notice the group and came forward to embrace her son. She hugged him tightly and asked him if he was okay. David nodded nervously. He could see the looks of concern on the faces of Ben and Sarah's parents; he appreciated it but also hated being the center of attention.

"David." His mother said softly. "I've asked Mr. and Mrs. Tolliver to come over because I'd like for you to still go away with them this weekend."

"Huh?" With everything that happened last night he'd almost forgotten that they were supposed to go to the cabin. He was torn though, part of him really wanted to leave but the other part wanted him to stay in case his mom needed him. He didn't know what they were going to do about his dad, but leaving just didn't seem right.

"I want you to go, honey. I think it would be best if you got away from this for a couple of days."

"But mom, I can't leave you. Not now."

"David, I've thought it over and Mr. and Mrs. Tolliver and Mr. and Mrs. Davidson agree it would be best for you; for all of you kids. It will also give me some time to figure out what I need to do." She pulled her son into another hug. "I let this go on for far too long and now I'm going to fix it. These next few weeks are going to be tough enough on you. I want you to enjoy yourself this weekend."

"Yes, David, your mother is right." Mrs. Davidson added. "I know you feel you need to be here with her but she will be okay. Mr. Davidson and I will see to that; we've already checked her into a room. Besides, she's going to need time to figure things out."

"Darling, please enjoy this last weekend of fun while you can. Please?"

As much as he wanted to protest he had to admit that he did want to get out of town and forgot about everything. He didn't have much time to contemplate though; his mother said the matter was settled and ushered him to his room to help gather his bags. Once in the room he noticed that his mother had brought more of his belongings.

"Mom, are you sure?"

His mom sat on the edge of the bed and patted the space next to her. He joined her and took her hand into his.

"I'm truly sorry I didn't help you sooner, David. I will never forgive myself for that." He tried to protest but she cut him off. "Last night; last night I finally found the strength to fight back. I know what I need to do. I'm leaving your father."

David was caught off guard; this sudden sense of determination in his mother was a surprise, a welcome one but still a surprise.

"I don't want you here though when I tell him. I need you safe and out of harms way. That's why I sent you here last night. I knew that the Davidsons and the Tollivers would help us." She kissed his cheek. "The next couple of weeks could be very difficult for us. Enjoy your time, please."

Before he knew it, he, Sarah, and Ben's family were packed into their SUV and on their way to the cabin. The drive was at least three hours and after an hour of talking Sarah and Ben occupied themselves with books while David opted for his iPod. The lack of sleep from the previous night was taking its toll and within minutes of starting a song his eyes closed heavily and sleep took over.

He dreamed he was hiking through a mountain side trail; he was alone and tired. The trail was growing dark and over grown rapidly; without notice the path was blocked with overgrowth. He tried to rip the vines and branches but he wasn't making any headway; the more he ripped the heavier the foliage grew. He tried turning around but discovered he was now surrounded on all sides. The brush began to harden and turn to stone and instantly he was inside a room that reminded him of his English class; then the room became his English class and he was seated at a desk. Mrs Chase wasn't at the front though, it was father.

His father stood before the class and began to write something on the marker board. David strained to see what he was writing; when his father moved David stiffened as he saw the word in bold black letters: FAGGOT.

"Class, today's subject is the faggot. You hate them. I hate them. God hates them. Everyone hates them; they are an abomination. However, what you don't know yet is that one of the people in this classroom is a genuine faggot. Yes, one of the wretched deviants has infiltrated your class. He pretends to be like you; he is not. He wants to convert you and your friends to his evil, wicked ways. He is an agent of Satan. We have to cleanse him and show him the true path to righteousness."

His father finally looked at David; his eyes were completely red, no other color could be seen.

"Class, you know what we have to do, right?"

All his classmates were staring at him and like his father, their eyes were blood red.

"Yes." They voiced in unison.

"What do we have to do?"

"Purge the evil."

"How do we purge the evil?"

"Kill him. Kill all the faggots." The group voiced.

His father pulled a gun from his pocked and pointed it David.

"Death is the only salvation. It is the only way to save you."

David tried to escape from the desk but he was now chained to it. He started pulling on the chains in a futile attempt to break them. His father inched closer and then the wall behind them exploded. A figure dressed in black swung into the room; with a swiftness he could barely see, the dark figure knocked the gun from his father's hand. A luminous golden rope shot into the room and engulfed the approaching horde of students lifting them into the air. David looked up to see the red, blue and gold outfit of Wonder Woman floating above the now ceiling-less classroom; however it was Sarah in the garb of the Amazon Princess. She gave him a quick wink as she pulled the gold tiara from her head and flung it at his chains, slicing through them easily. The tiara returned to Sarah's outstretched hand.

"Thanks!"

"All in a day's work." She winked again and rose higher into the air hauling the mass of students away.

David turned his attention back to his father; he was lying unconscious on the floor. He didn't see the dark figure who had subdued him. He inched closer, afraid he would wake at any moment.

"He will not hurt you again." A voice echoed from the shadows.

"Thank you, both of you. I don't know what I would have done."

A dark gloved hand touched David's arm and pulled him into a tight embrace. David was breathless as his body was pulled close and soft lips covered his own. It was like heaven; he felt every tingle of the dark knight's stubble.

"Good day citizen." He released David and inched back into the shadows.

David rushed forward. "Wait a minute . . . Batman isn't gay!"

"I'm not truly him." The deep voice lost its menacing tone and became softer, gentler, and more recognizable. A hand slowly pulled the cowl from his head and revealed the jet black hair and dark eyes of Ben.

David woke from his dream with a pleasant surprise. The dream had so many twists and turns; the comic book angle was interesting, however the idea of Sarah and Ben as his saviors was not that far from the truth. The ending though was a surprise; he and Ben kissing was the one thing he had always hoped would happen. He'd been in love with Ben since almost the moment he met him, but had never understood how deeply his feelings were until things with his father deteriorated. Thoughts of Ben

(and Sarah too of course) were what kept him going.

Sarah

Sarah bounced onto the bed relishing the fact that since the cabin only had three bedrooms and she was the only girl (aside from Mrs. Tolliver) she had one to herself. Ben's brother would be bunking with his parents while Ben and David shared the other room. This trip was exactly what she needed to rest; acres of land to explore, no neighbors, no Internet, and no television; nothing to distract them except for themselves. Sarah especially loved that there was no hotel staff constantly running around doing things she was more than capable of doing herself. Here she felt useful; helping unload the SUV, making dinner, and unpacking were things she never got to do at home. Surprisingly she loved doing them too.

Mr. Tolliver had cooked a delectable dinner of beef stew with fresh baked bread and they all gathered around the small rustic table sharing stories and conversation. She knew that she, Ben and David had dominated the conversation; making sure not to mention anything about the events of this morning. She could tell that Ben's brother Ryan was bored but Mr. and Mrs. Tolliver smiled and seemed to enjoy the show. She and Ryan washed the dishes and then joined Ben and David in a heated game of Trivial Pursuit; which seemed to last forever since none of them were able to get the brown chip so they gave up. She turned in feeling the weight of the day's events taking its toll. She had one final thing to do before allowing herself to sleep. She pulled the cell phone from her purse and tapped in Christian's number.

It rang only once before Christian answered.

"Hey sexy! It's the love of your life calling."

"Jenni! Thank God it's you. I was worried it would be Sarah calling again."

"Very funny."

Christian laughed heartily.

"Hi Sarah-bear; how was your day? I tried calling you at lunch but it kept going straight to voice mail. Did the terrific trio have too much to talk about today?"

She knew she'd forgotten to call him this morning to fill him in on what was going on with David and by the time she did think of it they were already on the road. She didn't think it would be wise to tell him the story with David sitting next to her.

"Sorry. I wasn't in school today . . ."

"Skipping already? I'm obviously a bad influence on you."

Christian hasn't been a bad student in high school; in fact he had straight A's his entire four years. By his senior year he had enough credits to graduate by the second quarter but the school did not allow students to graduate early unless they were entering the military. Christian would attend his required composition class and many times would skip out of the rest to work on his photography in the dark room. Sarah always worried he'd get into trouble but he was so liked by the teachers they simply overlooked it.

"No, it was something else."

"What happened?" He asked with concern.

She shared the events of the morning, taking great care to ensure that she recalled each moment. Christian didn't say a word, even after she told him how David's dad wanted to kill his son; all she could hear was his steady breathing. After a moment of silence she could hear him clear his throat and attempt to say something.

"Oh . . . no . . . no fucking way." He finally managed.

"Yeah." It sounded stupid but she didn't have any real way to respond. "Ben and I were floored; I'm telling you Christian I have never seen David so scared before."

"I could only imagine he had to be."

"We've know David for how long; yet somehow we did not know this was going on." She took a quick breath and continued. "We all noticed the change in his dad. But David, he never acted different. His dad was doing all those horrible things to him. How did we not notice?"

Tears fells as Sarah finally felt the rush of emotions that had been building in her all day. She was angry, mad, and guilty; guilty for not seeing the signs of her friend's pain.

"Sarah? Sarah-bear? Please don't cry." Christian pleaded. "Sarah, David probably did a lot to make sure you didn't notice. If anything he was probably trying to keep things as normal as possible for his own sanity."

"I know." She sobbed. "I know your right but I feel so bad."

"Sarah, I know you. You're thinking there was something you could have done to help or stop it. In reality there wasn't anything you could have done."

"Christian! How can you say that? If I'd known I could have . . . um . . . I could have gone to the police, or . . . or . . ."

"Exactly. Sarah, you don't know what you would have done. Let's suppose you had gone to the police. What would you tell them? What proof could you provide?"

She couldn't answer him; ideas raced through her head, but as she thought of each one she found a flaw with it. This was different though, she knew what had happened; she would have handled it better, right?

"I don't . . . I'm not sure."

"What about David?" Christian continued before she could finish her thought. "How do you think he would have felt to know you found out before he could tell you? Or how *he* wanted to handle it."

She knew he was right. If she had found out she wouldn't have thought clearly about how to proceed; she would have rushed out and done something and probably made things far worse.

"You are there for him now, Sarah. That is the most important thing. His mom sent him to you and Ben for help. Give him the love and support now and stop worrying about what might have been."

The tears faded and though she felt more exhausted now, she felt more at peace. Talking to Christian had allowed her to see a different perspective; one she hadn't even considered before. She felt as if a weight had been lifted.

"You always know what to say. Thank you."

"Anytime Sarah-bear."

"I wish you were here. I could really use a hug right now."

"Just imagine my arms around you. I'm sending all my love and comfort to you. I'll miss you this weekend but I'm glad you're with the guys."

"Thanks. What are you going to be doing?"

"Don't worry about me; I've got some work to catch up on. Nic has agreed to be my test subject for my next project so I'll be taken care."

"Good. Tell Nic I said Hi.

"I will."

"I don't want to, but I think I should probably get some sleep."

"I know. Enjoy your weekend. Give Ben and David my best. I'll talk to you later."

"Luv you."

"I Love ya, Sarah-bear."

She held the phone to her heart for a moment; she imagined Christian holding her in his arms. She was glad to be with the guys but she really wished Christian was here too; she wished he could kiss away her tears and hold her till she fell asleep. She sighed softly, placed the phone on the bed-side table and turned off the lamp. She hoped her dreams would bring her sweet and gentle thoughts.

David

He was sure he would be asleep the moment his head touched the pillow, but he was wrong; thoughts raced through his head. He could barely stand to lie in the bed, he was so full of energy he kept moving and shifting. Watching Ben undress and change for bed had been almost more than he could handle; his only saving grace was that they were sleeping in bunk beds. He'd tried so hard not to stare but he couldn't help it. He thought that maybe they could spend some time talking but it seemed as if the moment Ben crawled into the top bunk he was asleep. He contemplated waking him but decided against it; Ben needed his sleep.

David pulled his iPod from his bag hoping that listening to some music would help calm him down. He barely made it through one song before he pulled the ear buds from his ears. Maybe he should read. He turned on the small reading lamp next to his bunk; it would give just enough light to read but not enough to wake Ben. He looked over the books on the desk but none looked appealing. He knew Ben would have brought some with him so he decided to borrow one of his. He opened Ben's bag and found a graphic novel at the top; perfect, David thought. He pulled the book out and as he was about to close the bag his eyes caught the sight of the cover on the next book, The Best Little Boy In The World. He picked it up and read the description. He gasped; it dealt with a young man discovering his homosexuality. What was Ben doing with this? David didn't care, he had to read it. He crawled back into his bunk and started to read.

Hours passed as David grew more and more engrossed in the book. His eyes started to give out around 4:00 am so he reluctantly returned the book to Ben's bag. He took great care to make sure it was in as exactly the same spot as he could manage in his tired condition. He hated to stop, but he needed to sleep or he would not be able to function tomorrow.

When his head touched the pillow this time, sleep did come quickly.

Benjamin

Saturday 7:00 am.

We made it to the cabin safe and sound though I was beginning to wonder if we were going to make it at all. I can still hardly believe the things I learned yesterday . . . how could I not know my best friend was suffering so much. It makes me so mad to know that his dad was such a fucking dickhead to him. What kind of asshole does that? I know it is stupid of me to feel that way, because I know that there isn't much I could have done to stop it but at least I could have given David some kind of support. I'm sure that we did without knowing it - but still.

He looks so peaceful right now. I'm glad because he was tossing and turning quite a bit before I eventually got up. I've been up for about an hour now and I know I shouldn't but I can't stop looking at him. I was worried he'd wake up when I climbed out of bed, but he didn't even stir. Even when I started writing I couldn't stop watching him. I know that I shouldn't be thinking about him in that way, especially now; I can't help it. David is going through some really fucked up stuff right now and I need to not be thinking about my own selfish desires. I should be supporting him.

Instead I keep being drawn to his face, especially at this moment when the sun, which is just barely breaking through the curtains; is highlighting the shape of his nose and lips. I want to touch him and feel the warmth of his cheeks.

Okay - I have got to stop now. This is stupid. He is in pain. I need to forget my own problems and focus on his. I can not do anything to hurt our friendship. I can't.

Oh David, why didn't you come to us and tell us what was happening? I could have helped spare you some of the pain you're going through now. I know that I could turn these thoughts around to myself and ask why I haven't had the courage to tell my best friends the truth about myself and for that I can not answer. I know that I will tell them sometime but when?

Why can't I stop thinking about my own problems? Is that bad of me?

Till later -

B -

David

He could hear the shower as well as a jumble of noises coming from the kitchen; the clanking of pots, pans, and silverware; the laughter of Sarah and Ryan; and murmurs of conversations. The smell of coffee and bacon lingered heavily in the air and his stomach grumbled in anticipation. He couldn't delay any longer; he opened his eyes and pushed the blankets off. He wrapped himself in his robe and joined the land of the living. Sarah was playing a game with Ryan, who was apparently winning as she kept saying "You cheated." and "This game is rigged.". Mr. and Mrs. Tolliver were washing dishes and cleaning up the remains of breakfast. They all stopped when they noticed him.

"Good morning, sleepyhead." Mrs. Tolliver announced cheerfully. "Come here and have some breakfast while it is still warm."

"It smells great!"

"How did you sleep, son?" Mr. Tolliver asked.

David felt giddy hearing him call him son. It has been so long since anyone had called him that, well not his mom, but any father figure.

"Good. I had some trouble getting to sleep at first but I read for a while and that helped."

"You probably needed all the sleep you got. You had a long day yesterday." Mrs. Tolliver placed a plate of hash browns, eggs, and bacon before him then added a glass of orange juice. "Do you want some toast? And let me know if want more. It will take just a minute to warm some up; we've got plenty left."

He shook his head no to the toast and indulged in the hearty meal; savoring each bite. Generally his breakfast included a bowl of cereal, a pop-tart, or something he could grab on the way out of the house. He always loved being with Ben's parents as they made sure each meal was just that; a meal.

He ignored everything going on around him and focused on the taste of his breakfast until he heard the bathroom door open. He couldn't help but glance across the room to see Ben exit. He had his robe on but it wasn't pulled completely closed. As Ben was toweling his hair dry, David could just see the small patch of hair on Ben's stomach; he felt himself stir. He forced his eyes back to his plate and mentally told himself to swallow the mouthful of eggs. The damage though had been done; he couldn't stop imaging Ben removing his robe and toweling the water from his body.

He couldn't stop his mind from going to places that he knew it should not. Finding that book last night only brought more questions; could Ben be gay too? The only way he was going to be able to stop thinking about it was to find out if it was true, but how? His only time alone with Ben would be tonight when they went to bed. Could he come out and ask or should he just tell him how he felt? If he was gay, would Ben feel the same way towards him? What if Ben had feelings for someone else, or worse yet, maybe he had a boyfriend already? This was crazy. There were too many questions and what ifs. He could drive himself nuts trying to think of them. Surely there had to be something good coming his way; hadn't he endured enough pain this year?

He finished his plate of food and handed it to Mrs. Tolliver as Ben emerged from their shared room. He caught David's eyes and smiled. Again, David couldn't help but notice how attractive he looked in his sweater, un-tucked shirt and jeans.

"He's finally awake!" Ben said.

"Barely; someone's snoring was enough to keep anyone up last night."

David's quick retort brought an even brighter smile to Ben's face. Even the rest of the group laughed.

"Very funny. Now are you going to get ready or are Sarah and I going to have to go without you?"

"I'll be showered and dressed before you can get those hiking books laced."

"I'm timing you." Ben said as David rushed past into the bathroom.

Benjamin

Sarah left her game with Ryan and joined Ben on the couch.

"He looks good today. He seems back to normal."

"Yeah . . ." Ben said softly. He had been watching David closely since yesterday morning; partly out of concern, but also because he was afraid that he was going to miss something. He desperately wanted to grab his friend and offer him some kind of support; though he also wanted more. He once again promised himself that he would not say or do anything about his own personal feelings that would compromise their friendship.

David

After they assured the Tollivers they'd have the SVU back before they had to leave for their business dinner, the trio began their ritual trek into town. The town had grown considerably each year since they had been coming; they could each remember the addition of the movie theater, mall, mini-golf, and the usual fast food places. Their destination today was the mall. They loved it because it was filled with some of the worst stores they had ever seen before; it did have some saving graces though, the FYE music store and the BD Book store. They would do some minor shopping but the ultimate goal of their visit was their annual game of Hunt.

The rules of Hunt were simple; they'd split up and hunt the mall to find the most horrific, gaudy, tacky and useless knickknack. They would share their finds and vote on the worst. The winner would buy the item and give it to one of the losers. The item would then travel between the three homes where it would be displayed until a time where it would be ceremonially destroyed. Over the years the items ranged from statues of creepy looking dragons or angels with crazed eyes, to driftwood sculptures or bad knock offs of Precious Moment figures. Sarah's finds were almost always the winner; she seemed to have an eye for finding the worst.

David seemed to have no luck on his scouting mission; nothing seemed bad enough. He thought he had found something when he saw a Lady of Guadalupe statute that had fiber-optic lights bursting from her chest but the price of $30 was far more than the rules allowed; their limit had always been under $5.00. There had to be something he'd missed, he couldn't go back empty handed. He double backed towards the entrance thinking there had to be something at one of the kiosks. Passing the bookstore he glanced in the window and then he saw it; he had almost walked right past. The item was a statue of a child reading a book with an inscription that read "Books Make It Fun". What made it funny was that half the child's head was missing. It had obviously been dropped and damaged. He ran inside and checked the price, $0.99; perfect. Could he have finally found the winning item this year? He was reveling in his confidence that he almost didn't notice Ben at the counter with a book in hands. David noticed the cover and was instantly intrigued. It had three teen boys on the cover and the title was Rainbow Boys. David's first impulse was to call out but at the same time he didn't know if the mall was the right spot to possibly have this conversation. He hid behind a rack of romance novels and waited until Ben paid for the book and left the store. Rainbow Boys, was it another gay book? He found a store employee and inquired about the book. They knew the book and led him to the teen section. David thanked them and began to read the description. Could this be another sign pointing him towards Ben? He returned the book to the shelf and left the store.

Returning to the meeting place he could see Sarah already smiling confidently. Ben sat looking calm and unassuming with a plain white plastic bag resting between his feet. They each shared their finds and once again they were all in agreement that Sarah had found the tackiest item; a statue of a clown holding a screaming child. They all hated clowns so it won hands down.

"I thought for sure that damn statue would win." David said once Sarah left to purchase the dreaded item. "How the hell does she always find the one thing that makes us all cringe?"

Ben laughed in agreement.

"I know, I think this game is getting too easy for her; she knows our tastes too well. Maybe we should make some changes to the rules; then again, why bother, she'd just beat us again."

"Maybe we could do clothes or something flammable; lit a match and it's gone!"

"That's no fun. We wouldn't get to spend the hours planning the items demise. I mean, come on, remember last year. We had so much fun making that raft of twigs and sending it down the river as Sarah sang that God awful song from *Titanic;* it was pretty sweet."

David remembered it well. "Sarah attempting Celine Dion was great, but nothing beat the year we got rid of the angel."

It took weeks of gluing and painting, but once the rocket they had purchased for its demise was completed they duct taped the dreaded angel figure to the rocket and sent it soaring. Unfortunately it didn't go up; the weight of the angel toppled the rocket and it sent flying sideways along the grass and into the road where a truck drove over it, smashing it into shreds.

"Oh my God that was the best!" Ben nearly screamed with laughter. "Remember the old man watching us? He thought we were really upset. The look on his face when he finally realized we were laughing was priceless."

"That was hilarious! He called us crazy and said we were twisted!"

"We are, aren't we?"

"I think so." David breathed deeply.

"I wouldn't want it any other way though. We have so much fun together." Ben said quickly.

"You're right. I wouldn't want it any other way either." David said eagerly. He wanted to say more, but at the same time he didn't want to spoil the moment they were having.

"What's up with you two?" Sarah announced returning with the winning item in hand.

"We're just reminiscing about the good times, Celine."

Sarah laughed. "Don't remind me."

"So let's see it."

With more dramatic flare than one of the models on The Price is Right, Sarah presented the $2.50 clown statue. The guys both agreed it was truly hideous.

"Since I won, I can't take it yet. So . . ." She paused dramatically. "Who should get to keep the lucky item first?" Her hand rubbed her chin as she pretended to weight the decision.

"Get on with it!" Ben interjected.

"I nominate . . . David."

"Sympathy vote!" He objected.

Sarah hid a snicker as she tried to appear offended by David's outburst. She placed a hand on her waist and rose her other as if she was taking an oath.

"I swear this decision was made completely free of bias. I happen to recall that at the last hunt presentation Ben was the recipient of the prize."

"She's got a point. I did have to put up with that nasty thing on my dresser for three months before either of you finally agreed to take it."

"Whose side are you on?" David said with fake hurt.

"Mine!" Ben said quickly. "As much as I would love to have the . . . um . . . nice . . . clown figure; I do believe that it suits you better."

He knew it was a losing battle. He reluctantly put out his hand and accepted the object of his dis-satisfaction.

"You know, Ben and I were thinking maybe we need to change some rules for this game. Maybe the first being the one about the winner not having to take it first."

With a flip of her hair, Sarah took a role of superiority. "Well, as soon as the two of you win, we'll consider it."

Ben nudged David.

"We could leave her here."

"If only, Ben. If only . . ."

The two ducked as Sarah started swatting at them. The group burst into another round of laughter, gathered their bags and left the mall.

Another successful game of hunt had been completed.

Nicholas

Nic turned the invitation over in his hands again, he'd read it about ten times already but he couldn't stop himself from examining it again. The invitation was crisp ivory stock with a rough ripped edge effect that had him wondering if he had accidentally torn it when he opened the envelope. The lettering was an elaborate script in bright red with silver accents; their senior class colors, of course. It made perfect sense that Carmen and Kevin would choose those colors for their wedding scheme; they had always adored high school.

When the invitation arrived his first impulse was to not even open it but to throw it away; however the impulse to see it was too much. When he noticed the handwritten message inside he was glad he had. His heart raced and his reservations melted.

Nic - I know it has been while since we've seen each other, however Carmen and I hope you can make it and share in our day. We've missed you and would love to see you

Kevin

He slid open his desk drawer and withdrew a small wooden box. He'd had the box since childhood and though its contents changed over the years the purpose of the box hadn't; it held his personal and sentimental items. Pictures, movies tubs, and other mementos that had special meaning

to him were kept inside. He pulled out the stack of photos and flipped

through until he found the one he desired. It was from tenth grade and

showed him and Kevin with their arms around each other's shoulders

smiling and making goofy gestures with their hands. It seemed a lifetime

had passed since it was taken. He sighed as the memories started to return.

Tenth grade, Nic joined the yearbook committee and was partnered

with Kevin Johnson; they had known each other in passing and run in the

same circle of friends but hadn't talked much before. Within hours of being

partnered they were talking music, friends, video games, you name it; they

discovered they liked the so many of the same things. Before they knew it,

they were always together hanging out both in and out of school. They

even got jobs together at the local deli. Other friends were left behind; they

were inseparable. If one was seen without the other, they were asked where

the other was.

Even as the boys started dating they did things together; double

dates and outings were the norm. Nic dated Carmen for a short time and

though it didn't last he knew it before they told him that Kevin and Carmen

started dated. Nic and Carmen both felt it important to remain friends; Nic

had already started figuring out his sexuality at this point so he was happy

his friends had found each other.

By their senior year of high school Kevin and Carmen were the sweethearts everyone envied. As Nic struggled to come to terms with his true self, Carmen's best friend Jenny seemed to notice the changes in Nic and started questioning him. When he didn't answer her in the way in which she wanted to hear she accused him of not being a good friend. Twice she came right out and asked him if he was, as she loved to say, a fag. Nic denied it but, noticed that Kevin seemed reluctant to say anything to Jenny in his defense.

Then "it" happened on an overnight trip for the yearbook committee. Kevin, Nic and the other senior members of the committee were allowed to go to an amusement park as reward for their hard work. Kevin and Nic were sharing a room and as they were lying in their separate beds watching a bad horror movie Kevin seemed to notice that Nic wasn't himself. He asked Nic what was wrong. Nic had enjoyed the day at the park and had managed to forget about the tension that seemed to be growing in his group of friends but now back in the hotel he couldn't help but think about it. He tried to play it off with the standard line of having lots of stuff on his mind; Kevin didn't buy it. Nic tried to say that Kevin wouldn't understand and was surprised when Kevin retorted by asking if Jenny's accusations were true. Without thinking he said yes. Kevin didn't seem surprised; he said that he thought about it once or twice before. He asked Nic if he had ever been with anybody before. When he said no, Kevin asked him how he knew. He replied that he just knew.

It was silent for a long time as the revelations of their conversation sunk in. Kevin then asked if Nic would be interested in trying something with him. Nic wasn't sure if they should but he realized that the mere mention of possibly having some form of sex was making him horny. He asked Kevin if he was sure and Kevin said yes; he had only stipulation though, he did not want to kiss. Nic threw caution to the wind and agreed. They stumbled a little at first but then anticipation took over and they both tried pleasing the other orally. Kevin stopped after a little while and said he didn't know if he wanted to continue. He asked Nic if he liked it and when Nic acknowledged that he did enjoy what they were doing Kevin asked him to continue but he said he didn't think he could do anymore.

They both didn't know what to say afterward and they struggled to find anything to say that wouldn't bring up what they had done. Nic was filled with anxiety; he knew for certain that he was gay but he was worried that he had just screwed up one of the best friendships he'd ever had. Kevin broke the silence and said he wasn't gay. Nic asked him if he was bothered by what had happened. Kevin said no. Nic asked if they were still friends to which Kevin replied of course they were. It was uncomfortable for the next couple of days and even though he said it wouldn't change anything, Kevin appeared to be avoiding him. After a week, Nic had to force a conversation between them. Neither wanted to lose their friendship so they agreed to ignore what happened and move on. Carmen didn't seem to notice the tension between Nic and Kevin and even Jenny was being more civil towards him. On the surface everything seemed fine, yet Nic couldn't help but think that Jenny was watching him more closely.

Then a couple of months later, it happened again. The yearbook staff were off on a weekend trip and Kevin and Nic were rooming together again. Nic could tell that something was on Kevin's mind and tried not to say anything but after awhile he couldn't help it and asked him what was he was thinking about. The moment he said it he knew that Kevin was going to say that he was thinking about their last overnight trip. Before he knew it, Kevin was asking him to please him again. He said it was impossible for him to sleep when he got excited unless he masturbated and if he was going to do that he might as well let Nic get some fun out of it. It went against everything Nic knew to be right and he felt bad about cheating on Carmen but he couldn't control his own desires for Kevin; he agreed. When morning came, nothing was mentioned. Kevin wouldn't say anything and they would pretend nothing happened.

After the first time, Kevin had begged Nic to promise not to tell anyone and he agreed. After this second time he couldn't hold it in any longer; he couldn't ignore it like Kevin could. The moment they were back home he called his friend Donna and begged her to meet him for dinner. The moment they were in the restaurant he broke down and told her everything. Donna wasn't surprised by Nic's admission; she had actually assumed something was going on between them for sometime. She was appalled though by Kevin's blasé attitude toward Nic and Carmen; she could understand how Nic let himself be swept up in the moment. She warned him not to focus on the possibility of a future. At first he told her she was nuts he knew it wasn't anything but sex but the more they talked he realized he had indeed been letting himself imagine a life of possible love with Kevin.

As the months flew by Kevin began to call him less and less; Kevin even quit the deli so they only saw each other at school. As they pulled away Jenny took advantage and began following him around school and questioning Nic as to what he did to hurt them. When he would tell her he did nothing, she wouldn't believe him. She started accusing him more of being a fag and asked if he tried to force himself on Kevin. He finally got fed up and told her to mind her own business and to go to hell.

When it got to the point that Kevin would only talk when he called him or approached him, he simply stopped trying. At their graduation he and Donna sat together since Kevin had made a point to tell him that it would be best if he didn't join him and Carmen because Jenny would be with them. After the ceremony, Carmen came over and congratulated him and Donna and said she missed him and wondered why they didn't hang out anymore; Kevin and Jenny did not come over so he didn't approach them either. They sent a gift to his graduation party and even Jenny signed the card. He tossed it into the nearest trash can; he didn't need their pity he told himself. Before he left the hall he went back and dug it out of the trash, took it home and opened it; it was a watch.

For weeks he moped around wondering what he did to deserve such hatred. Had Donna not come by almost everyday and forced him to get out of his room and realize what a full life he truly had, he didn't think he would have gotten over it. His heart had been trampled.

Nic returned the photo and the invitation to the box. His fingers gently touched the watch that also sat inside. He closed the box, completed the RSVP card and placed in the return envelope. He knew that Christian and Donna wouldn't agree with his decision, but he had to attend. He had grown so much since those days; his life was so rich and rewarding. He wanted to prove to himself and Kevin that he wasn't the little boy who blindly followed anymore.

Benjamin

They arrived back at the cabin with plenty of time for his parents to get ready and leave for their dinner engagement. After a quick meal they began a marathon game of Scrabble with Ryan; who had the advantage of being allowed to use words not necessarily allowed in the game. Numerous rounds later Ryan had gone to bed while they continued with new rules; one game was to create as many proper nouns as possible; another was slang. Their current game was suggestive and inappropriate words. Sarah's all seemed to take the form of different ways to describe body parts, particularly the penis.

"I think someone misses Christian."

She tossed several tiles at Ben. Sarah had never hid from them that she and Christian had a sex life; much to Christian's dismay. Ben could see the smile on her face and knew what he said had been true. He liked that Sarah trusted them with the things that she probably would be telling Stephanie; Sarah's best girl friend.

"There is more to our relationship than that!" She tried to sound hurt but couldn't help but burst out in laughter.

"Not much!" Ben tossed tiles back at her.

"Well, maybe I'll just have to find someone else to talk to." She sat up and assumed an aura of superiority. "I mean, its not like you or David for that matter, share anything about your relationships."

"Don't look at me, I didn't say a thing." David said innocently.

Sarah continued ignoring David's interjection. "It's been months since either of you went on a date. Come on, I need more than Stephanie sharing what she's doing with James. I can only take so much of that!"

Ben smiled at the mention of their friend James, he and Sarah had never been that close; he knew how hard it was for her to know that James was his and David's next closest friend and that he was now dating her next closest friend. Though smiling he was also trying to keep himself from throwing up. Sarah's comment about him not dating caught him off guard. He didn't want to think of the possibility of Sarah or David guessing the real reason he hadn't dated anyone. He ignored the fear and plastered a smug arrogant look on his face.

"I'm extremely picky." He lied. "I have to make sure the person I date will pass the best friend exam."

"Ben?" Sarah paused. "Do you really think that David or I would judge anyone you dated? Do you really think we are that shallow?"

Sarah's innocent routine would have fooled almost anyone, except for Ben and David. They knew her better than anyone; Ben recognized the slight infliction of humor in her voice the moment she started speaking.

"Of course not, Sarah. Why would I think that? Oh wait, do I need to mention You Know Who?"

"Psycho Karen!" David shouted with laughter.

"Oh my God, yes!" Sarah joined in the laughter. She and David huddled together as they began reciting the many signs of Karen's psychoness.

"She still follows Ben around like a lost puppy."

"Or how about after Ben broke up with her that she started secretly taking his photo. Every time we turned a corner there she was snapping away. She must have at least a hundred photos of him in her locker." Sarah added.

"Or how about how she calls him Benji even though he hates it."

"What about the time she wrote her name as Karen Tolliver over and over in her notebook and conveniently, oh I mean, accidentally left it in the band room for everyone to see."

"I wouldn't be surprised if she's got a "Karen and Ben: together forever" website."

"I think her Facebook page list her as married to Ben, too!"

Ben sat silent watching his friends volley back and forth with examples of Karen's apparent mental challenges. Normally he would join in, but he was trying to prove a point. He waited until they started to lose stream and were struggling to come up with new ideas.

"I did break up with her after a week. I can't help it if I am so desirable that its caused her to go a little nuts."

"Oh please." Sarah laughed. "What did you see in her."

"That's not important. However you have proven my point about the friend exam."

David and Sarah looked at each other for a moment, shrugged and started laughing again. "We know!" They announced in unison.

"We're sorry . . . we're sorry Ben." David tried to apologize between laughs. He took a moment to catch his breath and calm down before he continued. "Seriously. We've all had our share of problem dates."

"Yeah." He relented. "Unfortunately none as bad as Karen."

He didn't relish the knowledge that his ex was the winner of the worst date title, but at the same time he only had himself to blame. He had only gone out with her as a favor to James. Before he started dating Stephanie, James managed to snag a date with a girl he'd been eying for a while. However there was a catch, it had to be a double date because the girl would only go out with James if one of his friends would go with her best friend, Karen. The date had gone okay, but Ben didn't feel anything for Karen; in fact, she bored him. He agreed to a second date because he couldn't think of a good enough excuse to say no. Before he knew it a week had gone by and they had gone out 4 times, each with the same results. He told her that he thought it best if they stayed friends instead of dating and at first she seemed okay with it. Then the stalking started. He couldn't go anywhere in school without seeing her. If it wasn't the picture taking it was the surprise visits at work or home. The only plus that came out of it was that his friends saw first hand how enamored she had become and understood why he broke it off before anything serious happened.

"Okay; enough about the psycho and past dates. Let's think about future dates." Sarah said with far too much enthusiasm.

"Oh no." Ben sighed.

"That's right; we've got to start thinking about Prom. Its finally our senior prom and we've got plans to make."

"I'm going stag." David sighed. "Too much going on to even think about looking for a date."

"I think I'll skip it. I hate those dances."

"Ben! No!" Sarah protested. "This is our last prom; you have to be there. Christian is coming and David's going; you have to come too."

"Yeah, dude; you can't leave me to be the third wheel to the Sarah-Christian love fest."

"But . . ."

"You will come Benjamin Mitchell Tolliver! It is a tradition for the three of us!"

Ben ignored Sarah's stern motherly tone. "Sarah, I know that. Its just I . . . I don't know . . . I don't have the desire to put on a . . ." He paused before he said what he truly wanted to say. He wanted to say that he didn't want to put on fake smile and pretend to be happy with some date that he had absolutely no interest in.

"It wouldn't be the same without you there though." Sarah pleaded.

The only reason he went to dances in the past was to be with her and David. At the homecoming dance his date even complained that he wasn't paying enough attention to her. It was a useless battle; Sarah would keep on until he said yes. He would not take a date though; he'd go stag. In a way, since David was going stag they would be going together.

"Please Ben?" She continued her pleas.

"You know I will." He relented. "However, you owe me big!"

"Of course. Anything for you Ben."

"Excuse me for butting in, but how many things do you owe him for already?"

"Stay out of it David. You're supposed to be on my side."

"What?"

The two jokingly bickered back and forth for a bit longer until David finally raised his hands surrendering to Sarah.

"Sorry boys . . ." Sarah yawned. "As much fun as this has been, I think it is time I get some sleep. I'll see you in the morning. Good night."

"Sleep tight."

"Good night, Sarah." Ben said as she left the main living room and entered her bedroom.

The boys remained sprawled on the floor with the Scrabble board still between them. They attempted to play a few more hands of inappropriate words, but both grew more tired as the game dragged on. Eventually they both started yawning and agreed it was time to abandon the game. Ben collected the tiles and packed up the game. Even though they agreed they were tired he got the impression that David didn't want to turn in yet. Twice Ben could have sworn that David was watching him yet when he met his eyes they were closed. He picked up the Scrabble box and returned it to the closet.

Ben found himself drawn to his friend again; David had stretched out further and his hands were cradling his head and his eyes were closed. The steady rise and fall of David's chest and the barely there smile on his face drew Ben in. He allowed his sight to linger on the dimple in David's left cheek and the soft stubble above his lips; the lips he wanted to kiss so desperately. His eyes traveled lower to his Adam's apple and the few stray hairs pushing at the opening of his shirt. He moved lower again to the now exposed peach skin on his midriff; it took all his effort not to return to the floor and touch the exposed skin. Instead, he inched closer and focused on David's shoulder; he gently shook the shoulder until David stirred.

"What? Huh . . . oh sorry about that. Did I drift off?"

"Just a little bit. You seemed to be in an out of sleep a few times during that last round. Ready to turn in?"

"Yeah." David sat upright and stretched, raising his shirt again and Ben saw more of his stomach muscles. He looked away quickly; he was getting excited and didn't want David to notice. David rose and began to enter the bedroom, when he noticed that Ben wasn't with him he stopped. "You coming?"

"In a minute." Ben said. "I'm going to lock up and then hit the bathroom."

"Okay - night."

"Night."

He waited until David shut the bedroom door before checking the lock on the door and turning most of the lights off. He left one lamp on so it wasn't completely dark when his parents came in. He retreated to the bathroom, brushed his teeth and tried to not imagine what David was doing. He could just barely make out some movement in the bedroom; he decided to wait a little bit and give David time to change and settle into bed before joining him. Despite the desire to possibly find David in some form of nakedness; he reminded himself of his promise. He had to stop thinking of his friend in that way. He had to forget about his own feelings and focus only on David's; they were the priority now. Ben sat on the edge of the tub and tried to calm himself.

He waited about 10 minutes before he left the bathroom and slipped into the bedroom. The lights were off but the curtains were still open and the room was illuminated in a bluish tint from the moonlight. It was more than enough for him to see without turning on a light. He undressed and started to pull his sweatpants on when he heard David sigh.

"Shit!" He gasped as he spun and noticed that David was sitting up in bunk.

"Sorry; didn't mean to scare you." David said sheepishly.

"It's okay. I thought you were asleep." He finished pulling on his pants and pulled his shirt on. He looked at his friend and was taken aback by the sheer beauty. David was sitting Indian style on the bed and seemed to be bathed in shining luminescence. His brown hair looked as black as Ben's own hair and sparkled with blue highlights; the white of his t-shirt glowed as if a black light was projected on him. His skin also had a bluish tint as well. He looked celestial.

"It was funny, I could barely keep my eyes open out there but the moment I got in bed I got really restless." David said. "Would you . . . do you feel like talking?"

"Sure." Ben said softly; he'd been expecting them to talk. His parents had shared some of the details of David's abuse with him this morning while David slept and Sarah showered. He hadn't pushed David for details and knew that he would be sharing stuff on his own terms. Ben assumed he was finally ready to share it.

Ben joined him on the bed, taking extra caution that he was close enough to lend his support but not too close where their skin might touch.

"I need to tell you some things and it might be difficult for me . . . and you."

"Okay."

"I guess I'll start at the beginning . . . um . . . last year something happened . . . well maybe not happened, but I guess I learned something . . . it was when . . . when I was dating Lisa."

Ben nodded unsure why David's story was starting here. He focused his sight on David, smiled and tried to show how his support. He didn't want to look as if he was hanging on every word. David opened his mouth and closed it numerous times as he struggled to find the right words. Ben placed a brotherly on his shoulder.

"Take your time. You don't need to rush this."

"You see . . . Lisa and I were out one night and she kept trying to get me to go farther; she wanted us to have sex. I know that some of our friends have already had sex with their girlfriends. I mean come on, how many times has James told us of his conquests." David laughed nervously.

"Anyway, I knew that I should be excited by the idea but my brain seemed to be screaming for me to stop. I panicked when she pressed harder and I just said yes. As I undressed I noticed that I couldn't . . . well . . . it wouldn't . . . it wouldn't get hard. I tried, I tried to figure out a way to get out of the room, but Lisa noticed and started asking me lots of questions.

We started fighting and broke up."

Ben recalled the night. David had called him to tell him about the break up, but he never told him that they almost had sex; he merely said they had a huge fight. He also remembered that David didn't sound very upset either.

"I had a feeling I know why it happened."

"You did? What was it?" Ben asked.

"Um . . . well, . . . let's see . . . as I'm sure you know we're almost 18 and it gets hard at the drop of a hat sometimes, but when it really goes into action is when I think of . . . well, um . . . boys." He said the last word quickly and almost in a whisper.

Realization came slowly to Ben; it was if he hadn't heard David's last word; but the moment he knew what had been said he couldn't help but look away and smile uncontrollably. He still didn't know what it meant yet so he stopped smiling and met David's stare. He could see tears in his eyes, but he knew they weren't tears of sadness. David had just come out to him and Ben still didn't know how to react. He'd prepared himself for a completely different talk and with just one little word he found himself sitting next to the one person he'd been longing for, but he also knew he couldn't jump to conclusions. David didn't know he was gay too.

"The . . . there's . . .um . . ." Ben cleared his throat. "There's nothing wrong with that, you know."

David smiled now. He nodded his head and he slowly moved his hand to Ben's that still sat upon his shoulder. He lifted it and cupped it in his own.

"I know."

"That's good. I think . . . I think it's important that you don't feel . . ."

"No, Ben. I know too." David said sheepishly. "I saw you at the book store today, and I found the book in your bag last night."

"You did?" The smile returned.

"Yeah. Last night after you fell asleep I was restless, so I decided to read and since I knew you brought some books I opened your bag and found the Best Little Boy book. The moment I saw it I had to read it. I wasn't sure at first but then I saw you buy the book today and okay, yeah, maybe I am making the biggest jump in conclusions but . . ."

Ben shifted his hand so that his fingers could entwine with David's. This simple little gesture spoke louder than words. They both smiled and Ben started to giggle.

"So . . . so I'm not jumping."

"No. You are right." Ben tried to imagine what David must have been thinking since last night. As he thought of their conversations today he recalled that David had seemed to be looking at him more intently that normal. Ben just assumed it was because of all the stuff David had been going through.

"Why didn't you say something sooner? I . . . I mean, obviously, you could ask me the same question."

"Ben, I wasn't even sure that I would say anything tonight. It just sorta happened."

"I'm, I'm so glad that you did.

"Me too."

"So . . ." Ben looked at his hand that was tightly holding on David's. "Where do we go . . . I mean what does this mean for us?"

"I don't know. All I know right now is that I really want to kiss you."

Ben couldn't ask for better answers. All his fears and confusion melted; they would make it work.

"Me too."

Ben inched closer to David, he closed his eyes and their lips met. It was if an electric shock passed through him; he came alive and hungrily kissed David. David pulled him close and their arms wrapped around each other; Ben relished the weight and heat of their bodies; he felt protected. He didn't care if they ever left this room again. He was in heaven.

Sarah

Sunshine broke through the gauzy curtains illuminating the room brightly. Sarah tried turning over and even putting a pillow over her eyes, but the glare was too strong; the snow outside was magnifying the sun's intensity to nearly blinding. She reluctantly pushed the blankets away and sat up; she was not going to be able to get any more sleep this morning. She could hear movement in the cabin, most likely it was Mrs. Tolliver or Ben; they were the only ones who got up at the crack of dawn.

She pulled on her robe and left the brightness of her room and immediately welcomed the darkness of the hallway. Mrs. Tolliver noticed her and bade a "Good Morning."

"Hi, we the only ones up?"

"Yes, you know Ryan and Mr. Tolliver can't ever rise before 9:00 am; it's like clockwork. What brings you up so early?"

"The sun, actually."

"Oh dear Sarah; I totally forgot to warn you about those curtains. We should have put a quilt over the window or something."

She could see that Mrs. Tolliver was generally upset. "It's no problem, Mrs. T. I could have done it myself too. I guess I was just lucky it was cloudy yesterday."

"Well, we'll make sure it's covered tonight."

"Sounds good. So I'm surprised Ben isn't up yet."

"I am too. Especially here at the cabin, he's usually up before anyone."

"Yeah, I crashed around 10:30 and both Ben and David were still up then so I don't know what time they went to bed."

"Mr. Tolliver and I got back around 1:30 and didn't hear anything when we got in, but you never know. The walls in this place are pretty solid, they could have been up talking till the wee hours of the morning and we wouldn't have heard them."

"Probably!" Sarah laughed. "You know since I am up, I might as well wake them too."

"Sounds like a good idea to me."

Sarah returned to the hall and put an ear to the boy's door. She couldn't hear anything so she slowly turned the handle and inched the door open. It was much darker inside; she tiptoed to the bed. She looked into the top bunk and noticed it was empty. What? Was Ben up? She turned around expecting him to be at the desk watching her but he wasn't there either. He must have gone to the bathroom without her or his mom noticing. She might as well wake David then. She bent and was surprised to see Ben; he had his hands crossed across his chest . . . wait a moment . . . there were three hands - and two of the hands were entwined and . . . . David's ring.

"Oh my!" She slapped her hands over her mouth before another word could escape. She slowly backed out of the room with her eyes glued to Ben's face; she wanted to make sure she hadn't woken him. Back in the safety of the hall she closed the door and froze. Nothing made sense for a moment. She thought she had it all figured out but now . . .

"Did you wake them?"

"W . . . What?" Sarah stumbled as she realized Mrs. Tolliver was talking to her. "Oh . . . no . . . they looked too peaceful."

Mrs. Tolliver nodded and returned to reading her book.

Sarah hurried back to her room. She closed the door and fell against it. So it was true; David too. It was almost too much to take in. She had stumbled upon Ben's secret a couple of weeks ago. She had run out of paper in her notebook and had asked Ben to borrow some. He handed her his and as she tore a few sheets out she noticed a page written in speedwriting. She and Ben had taken the course together the year before, she was rusty, but she was able to read it. Ben had written "I am gay. I can not lie to myself anymore." She thought she had misread it, but as she skimmed the rest of the writing she knew she hadn't.

Since that day she had been trying to watch him for signs. She even tried to bring up topics that might make him feel comfortable enough to share this news with her. So far nothing worked. She even sought out help from Nic, but he simply reiterated Christian's stance that she should wait until Ben came to her on his own.

Now however, she knew without a doubt it was true. David however was something she had not even considered. Were they a couple and if they were how long had it been going on? They saw each other almost every day and she hadn't noticed anything suspicious between them. Of course, she thought the same thing with David and his father.

She didn't care if there were a couple, did she? No! She loved them like brothers, they are her best friends. She wanted them to be happy. She had to talk to someone about this. She grabbed her phone and dialed Christian's number.

It rang several times and she was about to give up when the phone finally picked up. She heard heavy, sleepy, breathing and then a groggy hello.

"Christian?"

"No . . . hold . . . on." It was Nic. Sarah felt bad that she had wakened him. She could hear him call Christian's name.

"He's in the shower right now. Can he call you back professor?"

"Nic, its Sarah."

"Oh . . . hey there." He pepped up.

"I'm sorry I woke you. I just needed to talk to Christian."

"For you Sarah, I don't mind being woken up at the crack of dawn. I didn't even recognize your voice; I thought you were the professor

Christian's working with on his showing. She's been calling at all hours of the day. Let me tell him it is you."

She heard him yell again, this time mentioning her name.

"He'll be out in a second. You okay?"

"Yeah, something happened and I really need some advice."

Nic laughed. "Well, you called the right place. Christian is the voice of reason around here."

Sarah giggled now.

"Good, at least I got you to laugh a little bit. So, it can't be all that bad. Here comes lover-boy."

"Thanks Nic!"

"For you, anytime. Bye."

Sarah adored Nic and wished she got to see him more often, but as much as she talked to him on the phone and as much as Christian talked about him, she knew what a kind soul he was. He always asked her how she was or how school was going; she knew he genuinely wanted to know.

"Sarah-bear?" Christian said almost breathlessly. She knew he had hurried to the phone. "Are you okay?"

She wasn't even sure how to begin. She had shared her suspicions with Christian before and they had talked about it extensively. Now that she actually had him on the phone, she was at a loss for words.

"Yeah . . . I'm okay. I really . . . I need to talk to you."

"Okay?"

Words began to flow from her before she even knew what she was saying. But then she realized she was going round and round without actually saying anything. She stopped talking for a moment and took a deep breath. She had to just say what she needed to say.

"Ben is indeed gay."

"Did he finally come out last night?" She could hear the excitement in his voice.

"No." She recounted her journey into the shared bedroom and the discovery of David's arm intertwined with Ben's.

"Are you positive that's what you saw?"

"Christian, I recognized David's ring; unless Ben grew a third arm and has the exact same ring as David."

"True. But Sarah, you still don't know for sure. For all we know Ben and David could have been talking and simply feel asleep in the same bed."

"Okay, I'll give you that. However, how often do you sleep in the same bed as your friends . . . AND . . . end up with your arms wrapped around them? Don't forget that they were also holding hands."

Christian didn't answer.

"What else could it be? Ben . . . and David are both gay."

"We've talked about Ben before and I know that he being gay

doesn't bother you. I'm assuming you'd feel the same way for David, but this is different. It's both of them and its possible they are a couple."

In all their talks she had never given any thought as to how she would feel if both her friends were gay, she only focused on Ben. What was the real issue here; the gay part was a non issue to her; some of her favorite people, Nic for one, were gay. Was it because of the way she discovered it and that they hadn't come to her yet?

"I think . . . I think it was the shock of seeing them together."

"That's understandable. I imagine it must have been quite a shock. Just be glad they were both asleep and that you didn't interrupt something."

"Christian!" She didn't want to even imagine walking in on them doing . . . doing it. What would she have said or what would they have done. Oh, she definitely didn't want to imagine that scenario.

"I should be happy for them - no I am happy for them. So why do I still feel as if something is wrong?"

She was happy for them. It was no different than if they had come to her and told her they were dating a boy, only instead of each of them finding a different boy they found each other. Actually it made more sense, this way she didn't have to worry about the possibility of not liking one of the boys; she already liked both of them. Still something bugged her; they found love and would want to spend time together exploring it. She realized what it was. If this was a new romance they would want to spend time together - alone. Would they leave her out?

"Sarah? Sarah-bear? You're awfully quiet. What are you thinking?"

She didn't want to admit to Christian that she was afraid this would break up the trio.

"Sarah, remember they haven't changed. You're still the terrific trio."

"I know." She voiced finally. "It's just . . ."

"It's just what, Sarah?"

"I don't want their being a couple to break up the group."

Sarah gasped as she said it aloud. The three of they had been friends for so long and depended on each other every step of the way. Now there was a major change in their dynamics. There was so much going on, especially with David's parents. She wanted to be involved and help. She didn't want this new found love to destroy that.

"Oh my God, Christian. That sounded horrible."

"Sarah, it's natural."

"Natural? Christian, how could I worry about myself and how this is going to hurt my friendships? I should be happy and supportive and . . . and . . ."

"Sarah!" Christian cut in. "You mean far too much to both of them. The three of you are closer than many families. The guys will always want you to be a part of their lives."

"Really?"

"Sarah? Seriously, you know the answer. It's just still new and hard to focus and think clearly. As I said, it is perfectly natural to focus on the "what ifs" first."

"What should I do? Do I say something? Should I wait until they come to me?"

"I wouldn't rush anything. I'd let them come to you. If you're right, they need some time to themselves. Give them your love, but more importantly, give them time to come to you and share this. Don't push it."

"You always know what to say."

"It will work out, Sarah. I promise."

"Thanks. I love you, Christian."

"I love you too."

"I should probably let you go . . . thanks again."

"You sure you're okay?"

"Yeah." She said softly. "I am okay."

Christian

Christian hung up the phone, dropped on his bed and contemplated the conversation he'd just had; it wasn't what he expected at all. After hearing Sarah's description of David's situation with his father yesterday, he imagined that her call moments ago would have been in regards to that. True, he had been expecting the call about Ben's sexuality to come sooner or later, but not after yesterday. When Sarah first started questioning if she had truly read what she thought she read; she became tireless in her investigation to see if she could bring him to admit it. She was calling, emailing, and texting him and Nic at all hours asking questions. Nic started calling her Nancy Drew and saying she was working on the Case of the Pink Triangle.

"Everything okay with Sarah?" Nic asked as he returned to their shared dorm room.

Christian offered a shrug and smile.

"Nancy has cracked the case." Christian laughed as he said the Nancy Drew analogy aloud.

Nic smiled, shaking his head in amazement. He had told Christian that he thought Sarah was grasping at straws when she first told them what she read in Ben's notebook.

"Really? How did he do it.?"

"Actually he didn't."

"Okay, what happened?"

"She walked into the bedroom this morning and found Ben asleep in David's arms."

"Oh my. So not only is Ben but . . ."

"David? Yeah. Apparently. But as I told her she still can't jump to conclusions with this."

"What? I thought you said she solved the case. Didn't they talk?"

"No." Christian sat up. "Don't you listen? I said she found them ASLEEP in each others arms. She didn't wake them."

Nic nodded. "Is she okay?"

"Yeah. She's fine with them being gay; but she's struggling with so many things at once. She's confirmed that her one friend is gay, discovered her other friend is too while at the same time discovering that they are apparently a couple; that's a lot to deal with. But I think she's more concerned that if they are a couple and perhaps this is new that they're going to want to do lots of things together, without her."

"That's natural."

"Oh, I know. I just know that Sarah isn't ready for them to change yet. They're still in high school with just a few months till they graduate; she's not ready to face the reality that they will be going in different directions soon."

"I remember feeling the same way when we were seniors. Obviously I never expected my life to change as drastically as it did, but at the same time I know how scary change can be to some people. I sympathize with her. Though with all her . . ." Nic paused and held his hands up and indicated quotation marks with his fingers. " . . . "detective work", she must have thought that something was going to happen sooner or later."

"Much, much later. Knowing Sarah, she probably assumed that once Ben admitted to her that he was gay, they would talk about it and discuss and everything would stay the same. In her mind we'd get married, David would get married, and Ben would have a partner and we'd all still be together. Her vision of the future has been marred. It will take a little time, but she'll be fine."

"I know. I'll send her an email later and let her know that I'm still available if she needs further gay related assistance."

Christian sat and eyed his friend with fake contempt. It was so hard not to laugh as he thought about Nic's announcement. He knew that Nic loved being able to answer Sarah's questions; he'd been worried that Sarah was bothering him when she started, but Nic assured him he liked it.

"Shouldn't you be leaving for class soon?"

"Trying to get rid of me?" Nic asked suspiciously.

"Yes, you're driving me crazy."

"Actually, yes. I'm leaving in a few minutes. Besides, I thought you were due in the darkroom about 10 minutes ago."

"Oh shit." Christian jumped from the bed, grabbed the rest of his clothes and started dressing and gathering his supplies. "I totally forgot."

"What would you do with out me?"

"Don't start!" He teased.

"Okay. I'll see you later. You still want me to come by after class to help sort through those photos?"

"That would be great."

The two left the room together. Nic turned and walked backwards as he and Christian started down the hall. "We need to make sure we find a good pic of me in those, otherwise you'll never win that grant."

"Oh, of course, the judges aren't going to care about my artistic take. They are only interested in the subject matter. Is that it?"

"Absolutely. The subject is the . . ." Nic couldn't finish as had walked right into a trash can, tripped and fell to the ground. Laughter filled the hall as other students saw what occurred and joined Christian in his amusement.

"If I only had my camera out. I'd have the perfect shot."

Nic accepted Christian's hand and stood from the floor. "Fuck you." He joked.

"You wish!"

"Not in a million years; you're not my type. I don't like twinks."

"Oh right, you like them burly and hairy."

"Nothing wrong with a little hair; I'm sure Sarah would agree - oh wait, you don't have any. How does she stand it?"

"Get out of here." Christian punched Nic's shoulder.

"See ya later."

Christian stood a moment and laughed as he watched his friend saunter off towards his class. He and Nic hadn't known each other very well in High School but they were both glad to have least known of the other when they had been assigned as dorm mates. Christian knew quickly that he had found a true friend in Nic.

A thought suddenly occurred to him. Sarah adored Nic, maybe the guys would too and maybe, just maybe, he could be an inspiration to them. He pulled out his phone and dialed.

"Sarah. It's me. Listen, I just had a great idea."

Benjamin

He tightened his grip on David's hand, he didn't want to let go, it was if they released he would wake up and realize that last night was a dream; though he knew it hadn't been. They had literally spent the entire night wrapped in each others arms. He always imagined that when he finally did get to sleep with someone they would fall asleep like this but would wake up on opposite sides of the bed. Like a single unit, when one moved the other matched it. Ben relished the warmth and strength of David's arms; he felt safe.

His fingers traced the knuckles on David's hand and played with the ring on his thumb. Their hands were similar however this was new territory; David's skin was smooth in some areas and course and rough in others. Ben could feel the patches of roughness that had developed from David playing the drums. For a moment he considered exploring more and almost regretted that that they hadn't done anything beyond kissing last night. But the anticipation of being able to feel David's breath on his neck again and the ability to spend hours exploring each other was more than he could hope for. He didn't care if it took months for them to go further as long as they could kiss and touch, that meant more than anything.

His stomach quivered as a soft kiss touched his neck. David's other hand was now gently combing through his hair. Ben let a sigh escape his lips. Their hands untangled and David gently stroked Ben's exposed stomach. He wanted to wake up like this every morning.

"Morning." David whispered in his ear.

"Morning." Ben responded. He shifted so he could be face to face with David. He stared longingly into David's green eyes and let his fingers trace his cheeks. "How did you sleep?"

"Great."

"Me too." Ben was glad he had thought to close the curtains last night or he would have woken much sooner and he would not have been able to savor the time in David's arms as long as he had.

"I wish we never had to leave this room."

"Yeah. I've been up a little bit myself. I didn't want to let go."

Ben's fingers danced across David's cheek and traced the lines of his lips. David reciprocated with running his fingers through Ben's hair and gentling pulling him closer until their lips met. They hungrily embraced and attempted to kiss and explore with the same eagerness as last night, but both seemed to know they had to be careful not to arouse the attention of the other occupants of the cabin. Numerous times they each had to cover their mouths to muffle the moans of pleasure that were trying to escape.

"Ben . . . Ben . . . stop!" David gasped. "We're going to get caught."

Ben winked and arched his eyebrow. He knew David didn't really want him to stop, but he knew he was right.

"Sorry. I'm just having too much fun. I don't want to let you go."

"I'm not going anywhere."

"Good." Ben returned his hands to David's chest. "You know what I would love to do?"

"I could probably guess a few things." He smirked. "However, I'll ask anyway. What would you like to do?"

"Take a shower."

David pulled away and looked sad. "No one's stopping you."

Ben pulled him back and kissed him. "No dumb ass! I would like to take a shower with you!"

David's eyes widened in delight; Ben knew he wanted to do it as much as he did. Their situation however made it impossible; his parents and Sarah would surely notice that.

"Sadly, I think it best if we took separate showers." David and Ben sat up and untangled themselves. "I don't think your parents would be too keen on their son and his male friend sharing a shower. We can't let your parents know. Who knows what they would do. Believe me you don't want to find out!"

Ben realized instantly what David was telling him. Everything made sense now; his dad wasn't mad that he had been masturbating, he was mad that David was gay. That's why he freaked out so badly.

David started to stand and Ben reached out and grabbed his hand.

"Ben, we have plenty of time for kisses later, we should probably start getting . . ."

"He knew!" Ben interrupted.

"What?" David said confused.

"He knew! Your father; he found out you were gay. That's what set him off."

David froze as if he'd been hit. His face went pale and his eyes started to tear up.

"David?"

He couldn't answer verbally, he was trying not to cry; he simply nodded yes. Ben jumped from the bunk and hugged him. He kissed his cheeks and whispered assurances to David.

This had been the one fact that David had not been able to share before; now that it was out in the open it was affecting him strongly. Ben often wondered how his own parents would respond when he finally told them the truth. They had never been a very religious family so he was confident they would not use that against him. He liked to imagine that they would support him. He knew they would be scared for him because of people's prejudices; but they had told him and his brother many times that they would love them no matter what. He knew that would be true for this as well.

He knew Sarah and Christian would be fine too. Christian was the coolest straight guy he had ever met; they had many talks about politics, religion, and other world problems and Christian was always one to mention the injustices placed on gays during those talks as well.

"I'm sorry Ben."

"For what?"

"I didn't want you to find out like that. I wanted to tell you the truth . . . but I just . . . I couldn't say it aloud. Then with everything last night . . . I didn't want to spoil it."

"You didn't spoil anything. I can't begin to imagine what you must have been going through."

"Pretty fucked up, huh?" He pulled himself from their embrace and sat on the edge of the bed. He looked up at Ben, smiled and then dropped his head into his hands. "My life is so screwed up."

Ben knelt before him, placed his hands on his shoulder and kissed his head.

"I know this seems bad now, things will get better. I promise."

David raised his head and through teary eyes, he smiled brightly.

"Hearing you say that, I almost believe it."

"Believe it. I'll do whatever I can to help you through this David."

"I know you will. I don't know if I can handle this without you."

Ben kissed David's lips and hugged him. He wanted him to know that he would give him as much support and love as humanly possible. The next couple of weeks were going to be hard for David, if he could at least provide him some joy and love that was something. Again, he wished they never had to leave the cabin, here they could forget everything and be happy; but Ben knew it also wasn't realistic. They had to return to the real world and find a way to keep their love strong.

PART TWO

Benjamin

He opened his locker, dropped his books inside and grabbed his phone; no messages. Damn! He'd been waiting to hear from David all morning and it was making him more nervous by the moment. Since their return from the cabin a month ago David had been meeting with more people than he had ever imagined possible; the police, his mother's lawyer, social workers, and now today was the first meeting between his parents and their lawyers. Though he wasn't required to be there, David had requested to attend. Last night when they had been studying David admitted to being scarred to see his father again. His mom had been sheltering him from his father but since starting divorce proceedings and the multiple visits from the police, his father's anger seemed to be beyond the boiling point. During the first week he phoned the hotel constantly wanting to speak to David's mother and when she wouldn't take his call he became verbally abusive to the staff. Another visit from the police ceased those calls and he began consenting to changes.

Despite the problems with David's father, it actually had a positive outcome for Ben; David was showing up at his house at all hours of the day; most times it was under the guise of studying but mainly it was for moral support. Sometimes he would share some stories about the torment his father gave him, sometimes he'd just want to be held, other times he wanted to kiss, and then there were the times he'd come over and simply fall asleep from sheer exhaustion. Even when Sarah was present he would crawl into Ben's bed and sleep while Ben and Sarah talked. At school David seemed to seek them out more often. It seemed to be his pick up for getting through school and the issues at home. At first Ben didn't think he was helping much, but seeing the smile on David's face as he slept or the twinkle in his eyes as they kissed, he knew that in some small way he was.

When David told them he was going to accompany his mother to the lawyers today, Sarah thought he had cracked. She couldn't understand why he would want to go and see his father again; Ben agreed with her. David said he had to be there for his mother, and while Ben believed him he also thought that perhaps David was also going for another reason. Ben believed David had to prove to himself that he could look at his father again.

Ben returned the phone to his coat pocket and grabbed his lunch; Sarah should be here any moment.

"Hi Benji!"

His hair stood on end as the sickeningly sweet voice of Karen echoed through the hall. His mind raced with ideas of escape but it was impossible; she was too close for him to pretend he didn't see or hear her. She rocked back and forth on her heels. He gave her a fake smile and nodded with disinterest, hoping she would get the hint that he didn't want to talk; she didn't, she rocked faster. His stomach turned.

"Benji! How are you? It's been, like, forever since we've talked."

Benji! God how he hated it when she called him that. He'd told her that about a million times, but like many things he'd said to her, she seemed to not hear it or to ignore it.

"I've been busy Karen." He tried to sound short and annoyed, which wasn't hard. She seemed oblivious to his mood.

"I know! Senior year takes up so much time. I mean, like, studying and planning for exams and then, like, all the prep work for college."

"Yeah . . . whatever." He checked his watch. What the hell was keeping Sarah. She was going to pay for this.

Karen hugged her books to her chest and smiled nervously.

"Benji . . . are you . . . are you, like, going to . . . you know . . . prom?"

No! This was the last thing he needed or expected from this conversation. What the hell was Karen thinking? They broke up almost a year ago. He never talked with her or more likely he never instigated a talk with her. Why couldn't she get the hint; he didn't like her. He wasn't sure what to do. Could he just tell her to get lost? No, sadly, he wasn't that type of guy. Maybe he should tell her that he wasn't going or maybe he could tell her who he was going with. That would certainly blow her mind and solve the problem. No, that would only bring up more problems and he and David had enough to focus on right now.

"Look, Karen . . ."

"Sorry I'm late Ben, but you wouldn't . . ." Sarah rounded the corner nearly plowing into Karen. "Whoops!"

Karen didn't acknowledge Sarah's arrival; they had not been friendly at all during the short time she and Ben had dated. Sarah shared a questioning glance with Ben. He rolled his eyes in answer.

"Am I interrupting something?" Sarah asked playfully.

"No!" Ben said quickly before Sarah could continue her attack. He turned his attention back to Karen.

"Karen, I don't think it would be . . . fair . . . to either of us to go backwards. Its over, let's leave it at that."

"Benji." She lowered her voice and tried to speak only to Ben. "I know things didn't work out before, I think we both know there is something between us still. I feel it."

"You're the only one that does." Sarah whispered under her breath.

Ben shot Sarah an evil look. He knew what Sarah was doing; she was trying to bait Karen into a discussion so she could smack her back down. He'd known Sarah long enough to know that there were only a few people in the world that irritated her so much that when the opportunity arrived she couldn't help but come out with fists swinging. Karen was at the top of that list. However, today was not the day. There were more important things to focus on.

"No, Karen. There is nothing. Please stop believing there is more here than there is or was."

"But Benji . . ."

"It's Ben!" He said angrily and then immediately calmed down. "I'm sorry. But I can not do this today. Please, not today!"

Karen finally acknowledged Sarah with a quick glance.

"Of course, your buddy is here. You're not about to, like, talk about us with her here. Bye, Benjamin."

She pushed past Sarah and entered the lunch room.

Sarah didn't say anything, she waited until she and Ben had walked to their favorite lunch time spot; the stairwell. Ben knew it was killing her not to say something about Karen, he was just thankful she waited until he had at least started eating.

"So . . . Benji, I see the crush is still in effect." She teased.

"Oh my God! What did I do to deserve this?"

"It could be worse."

He knew she was right and he was grateful it wasn't; he could handle Karen. There were far more important things to worry about, namely David. It had been all the two of them talked about on the drive to school this morning. They'd been to his locker between every class checking to see if he'd text yet.

"Any news?"

"No."

"Let's hope no news is good news."

Ben wondered how Sarah would be handling the situation if it was Christian going through this. He hated that she would be able to share her true feelings; she would be able to be openly upset. She would be able to hug him, hold his hand, and kiss him without fear of abuse. She wouldn't be sneaking supportive touches and winks like he had been doing with David. The only time they could hold hands in school was during Chemistry since their lab table was at the back of the room and completely hidden from direct view. He was envious of the public displays his straight friends took for granted.

"What do you think is going on?"

"Huh?" He realized he hadn't been listening to Sarah.

"I said, what do you think is going on right now?"

"I have no idea. I keep imagining them sitting across some large table hashing out details. I also keep imagining Mr. Whitman spitting curse words at David."

"Me too."

"I wish we could have gone with them."

"Yeah, I still can't believe Mrs. Whitman and David are moving back into their house today. When she told mom that Mr. Whitman agreed to give her the house, I thought it was a trick. David and his mom both said they were anxious to go back home, but I don't know if I could do it."

"I was surprised by that too. After hearing what David told us; if it was me, I don't know if I could sleep in that room again."

"I'd be scared to death. The only good news is that Mrs. Whitman is having the locks changed and that security system installed."

"Well, at least in a way, things will be getting back to normal."

They finished their lunches and took their daily walk around the halls until the bell ending lunch sounded. They returned to Ben's locker and checked his phone; there was a message. Ben held the phone so Sarah could read the message as well.

Out of mtg. Very weird. Details later - police escorting us home. Come by after school. D

Ben said a silent prayer of thanks. He'd been so nervous that something bad was going to happen. At least the first hurdle was complete and most importantly, David was okay.

"Thank goodness." Sarah sighed. "Well, I am off to history. I'll see you after school and we can drive over to David's together."

"Cool. I'll see you in two hours."

Ben grabbed his chemistry book and headed for class. He didn't like having to be there by himself, but he knew it was only a short time before he could escape and see David. The only down side was that Sarah drove today so he wouldn't be able to stay late and give David any boyfriend support. He realized that was the first time he'd actually thought the word; but that was what he was, he was David's boyfriend. At least they would be able to spend tomorrow together as Sarah was heading up to spend the weekend with Christian. He couldn't wait; he had so many plans for them. First they would . . .

"Ben Tolliver?"

He was pulled from his thoughts and realized he'd made it all the way to chemistry class and took his seat all while being completely lost in thought. The bell had even rung and class was started.

"Mr. Tolliver would you please open your book and join the class?"

"Oh yeah, sorry Mr. Vito."

The hour crawled by as Mr. Vito made a point of calling on Ben more than any other student in the class. When the bell rang he grabbed his books and rushed out of the room before Mr. Vito could hold him back and express his disappointment with Ben's lack of attention. Mr. Vito was famous for doing it and Ben wasn't willing to give him the opportunity.

He arrived early for his final class, which thankfully was also his favorite - Band. He was in his seat and warming up his saxophone long before anyone. He missed being able to see David in the back of the room with the rest of the percussionists, but he pushed the disappointment away and focused. He played with such determination and concentration that the hour flew by. As he packed up his sax, James stopped by.

"Great playing today dude. What the hell happened; normally you suck!"

"Very funny!"

"So where the hell is David? Chuck and I thought the four of us could go and get some burgers and then hang out and play some PS3. It's been a week since I had the chance to kick your asses."

David had asked him and Sarah not to share with their other friends what was going on with his parents. They understood and had both agreed they'd tell people he was sick. He played it up more than he probably needed to by saying things like David was up most of the night throwing up: he didn't want to just say David wasn't feeling well.

"That fucking sucks. Stephanie was out a couple of days ago with something like that. I hope he doesn't have what she had; though I'll tell you it didn't stop me from kissing her." James nudged Ben knowingly and laughed. "But you know, he did look a little out of sorts yesterday."

"Yeah. So the ass kicking will have to wait. How about you give us a call tomorrow? Sarah is heading out to see the BF and as long as David's feeling up to it he and I were just going to hang out. Maybe we could get together in the afternoon?"

"That sounds good. Steph's busy tomorrow too. I'll check with Chuck and see if he's free. We'll give you . . . oh no . . . Psycho alert."

"What?" Ben turned slightly and noticed Karen inching towards him. She had her flute case in hand but instead of heading to the instrument storage room like everyone else she was watching him and James.

"Sorry dude, but I think she's heading your way."

"Damn. Not again."

"If you'd like I could tell her to fuck off for you?"

Ben laughed and appreciated the support of his friend.

"No. Its okay, I'll take care of it. Give me a call later and we can discuss tomorrow."

"It's a plan. Go get her."

Ben picked up his case and moved to the storage room ignoring Karen. He didn't have to look to know that she was following him. There was only one entrance so he knew he was trapped. He pushed his case into his assigned slot and attempted to leave.

"Benji?"

"Look!" He said more harshly than he intended. He took a quick breath and tried to remain calm. "Karen, I am not about to get into this now. I'm going home."

"Benjamin, please wait a minute. I know that, like, you only said those things because Sarah was there. I want us to be, like, friends and you know more than that too. I know that . . ."

Before she could finish several of their classmates entered the room and noticed them. They laughed out loud and then apologized to Ben. After they placed their instrument cases in their spots and started to leave, Ben could hear one of them whispering about Karen. He couldn't hear everything they were saying but the word loser was clearly audible.

"I am only going to say this once. First, my name is Ben, not Benji; do not call me Benji. Second, I don't think we can be friends. You've made that clearly obvious. There is nothing, I repeat, nothing between us. Good bye."

More classmates entered the room and Ben used it as a diversion to escape before Karen could say another word. He ran from the band room to the first exit he could find; he wanted this day over. Twice in one day was a new tactic for Karen. Normally after one interaction she would avoid him for days, sometimes weeks. He hoped today was a one time occurrence; he couldn't deal with this on a daily basis.

He found Sarah already waiting in the car with radio blaring.

"Let's get out of here, please." He said the moment he opened the door.

"Your wish is my command." Sarah said. "Let's go see David."

Nicholas

"How do I look?"

Christian looked up from his laptop and gave Nic a quick once over. Nic had already bothered him about five times in the last half hour as he kept changing his attire. He'd tried on his new suit first and Christian had told him he looked sharp, but Nic changed the shirt and then the tie and couldn't decide which one looked best. Now he gave up on the suit and was trying his sport coat.

"You look good."

Nic sighed audibly. "I know you are straight, but couldn't you have at least one little thread of metrosexuality in you. Sharp. Good. Nice. Great. I need more than that."

"Sorry, I missed that craze. Anyway, what's up with the different jacket?"

"You just noticed that now?"

Christian shrugged his shoulders in question.

"You are hopeless. To bad Sarah won't be here tonight, at least she'd be able to help me."

Christian sat back in his chair. "Why are you so worried about what you are going to wear? Its just a wedding. Okay, okay . . ." He held his hands up as if he knew Nic was about to tell him it wasn't just a wedding. "I mean, I thought that is why you bought the suit?"

"It is, but then I started thinking that maybe it was too much."

"Look, I know this wedding means a lot to you and that you want to show your old friends how well you are doing, but why are you driving yourself crazy? The suit was perfectly fine the way you had it at the beginning. Is it really the clothes you're worried about?"

Nic knew what he was getting at and he had to admit that Christian was right. Nic was letting his own fears about how Kevin and Carmen would react affect him. As much as he loved to say that he didn't care what they thought, that wasn't exactly true. He wanted them to know that he was happy, secure, and at peace. He wanted them to know that he forgave them for the way he was treated; they had all been young and stupid then.

There was one thing that he had never admitted to anyone before and that had been playing in his thoughts lately. There was still some small part of him that still felt *something* for Kevin; but what that something was, he didn't know. He knew that it wasn't love, but it wasn't hatred either. The mention of Kevin's name or a glance at an old picture brought out some emotion in Nic that he couldn't explain. Sometimes he would feel longing, while other times it was anger, and sometimes he even felt like running. There was something there and it terrified him to admit it.

Why was he letting this enigma of emotion control him? He hoped that seeing Kevin again would answer that question.

"I know your right! I don't know why I'm freaking out."

"It has been some time since you saw them and with everything that happened between you and Kevin I imagine there must be a small part of you that wants to rub their noses is how good your life has become since high school."

Nic thought about it for a moment and knew it was true. Sure, why not be proud and let them know how good his life was. Sure he was still in college but he would be graduating soon in the top of his class and had been receiving lots of inquiries of employment from numerous companies. Plus, he had a fantastic group of friends who treated him with love and respect. Why shouldn't he want to brag a little?

"I'd be lying if I said you were completely off base." Nic admitted. "But that's not the real reason . . ."

"Nic. I know that."

"You don't think I'm crazy to go, do you?"

"No, I don't. If anything I think I can understand; its not about rubbing their nose in it or even wanting to see how much you might still have in common. Unless I'm completely off base, and after the many, many stories you've told me about Kevin; I think it has to do more with closure."

Nic was surprised by his comment. Closure? Was that what he wanted?

"Think about it, Nic. You're relationship with Kevin hit a wall and instead of dealing with it and actually clearing the air and moving on, it simply stopped. You didn't have any say in the matter. You're going to finally close the door on that chapter of your life and continue moving on. If, by some odd chance a new door opens, so be it."

"You're right. I never thought of it in that way before though." Nic smiled and then laughed. "Would you mind telling Donna that so she'll finally agree to go with me?"

"No. You're on your own with her. I know better than to even attempt to change her mind."

David

His bedroom was in shambles; clothes ripped to shreds were strewn everywhere, the dresser drawers jutted open with more ripped clothes spilling out. Pictures ripped from frames and albums were torn, burned, and marked out now littered the floor along with shards of glass and other debris. A baseball bat sat in what had once been a 17 inch television. His mattress had been pushed off the box spring and now held a black spot in the center where he could only a guess a fire must have once burned.

He'd scanned the room several times and still couldn't find a single item which hadn't been destroyed; even the smallest of objects like paper clips were mangled. Pictures of him and his late grandparents had either his face cut out or marked over in permanent ink. The frame of his closet where his mother had made hash marks to chronicle his growth over the years had even been yanked from the walls.

His mother had simply stood horrified when she first saw it. David had to literally pull her into the hall and walk her to her own room. Once she was lying down on her bed he examined the rest of the house. The living room looked the same except for the blank wall that his school pictures once occupied; he assumed the lump of burnt glass and wood in the fireplace was where they met their end. The kitchen was untouched, but the bathroom had both mirrors smashed and his allergy medicine was dumped into the toilet with what he could only assume was his father's urine. David shut the lid and flushed it away. He almost wished that the police had checked the house when they dropped them off, but since the front room looked fine he and his mother assumed everything else would be fine. How wrong they had been.

He returned to the kitchen and grabbed the box of garbage bags; he had to get rid of everything. Returning to his room he felt a wave of hot tears start, but he held back. He couldn't give in to them. He had to stay focused; he wanted the room clean and fresh for this evening.

He dumped everything to the floor and started filling bags. He was so engrossed with cleaning that he didn't hear the doorbell or his mother walk by to answer the front door. It was the sound of Ben's voice that broke his concentration. He could hear his mother saying something about David being strong and brave. Sarah's soft laughter came now and his mother's warning that things weren't good in his room.

That wasn't true though, he thought. For the first time since this ordeal began he realized his fear was gone. He didn't care if his friends knew the full extent of his father's anger and hated. This room, this trash was just stuff; it was stuff he could easily replace. The important thing was that he was safe and loved. He had the love of his mother, Sarah and most importantly, Ben. That was more than he could ask for.

David met Sarah and Ben at the entrance to his room; both were wide eyed and silent. Neither of them seemed sure how to respond to the extent of the damage.

"It's okay guys. Really . . . I'm okay."

Ben stopped staring at the room, gave David a wink and placed a hand on David's shoulder. He didn't let it linger long before he removed it. He entered the room, grabbed a garbage bag and began to pick up trash.

Sarah on the other hand looked as if she needed some coaxing to move.

"Sarah, come on in. It's not as bad as it looks. I mean, sure nothing is salvageable, but I've got plenty of clothes and many of the pictures were scanned and are on my laptop. It's all replaceable."

"My God, David. I can't believe it. How . . . how can . . . you stand there . . ."

"Don't." He said softly. He didn't want this to be about his father. "Please, don't say anything. It's . . . it's okay."

"All right." She offered a smile. It was a weak and he knew it was forced but at least it was a smile.

"We'll help you get this place cleaned up." Ben offered in his most sincere voice.

Sarah

Laughter filled the desolate room and she saw the genuine smiles on Ben and David's faces. His father had utterly destroyed everything in David's room, but having his friends here was more than enough to bring a smile to David's face. She took David's hand and placed the small clown statue from their most recent game of Hunt in it.

"Here. No ceremony or fuss. Let this be your first new item."

David tried to not burst out laughing.

"I'd say thanks, but you really shouldn't have. Seriously! Seriously, you shouldn't have."

Watching her friends laugh a realization struck Sarah. Her fears about the guys pushing her aside so that they could focus on their budding romance were wrong. Her friends would always be there for her just like she would always be there for them. It didn't matter that Ben and David were a couple; the friendship the three of them shared was strong enough to conquer any of her fears.

She noticed the quick glances between Ben and David and knew she wanted them to have some time together.

"Oh." She tried to sound shocked. "I totally forgot I promised to run some errands for my mom. I need to get home or she'll kill me."

"Really?"

"Oh yeah, I'm sorry David. Hey, could you take Ben home later, that way he doesn't have to leave now?"

"Um . . . sure . . . I'll take him home."

She hugged each of them and surprised them by kissing each of their cheeks. She hurried from the room and got back into her car. She could see the confused looks on their faces as she pulled out of the driveway; she waved and gave her most convincing smile. She waited until she was out of sight before picking up her phone and dialing Christian's number.

"Christian! I know . . . you're in the dark room, but I had to tell you that you were right. Everything is going to work out . . . everything is going to be okay."

Benjamin

Between the two of them twenty bags of garbage were carried to the curb; along with a mattress, a television with a baseball bat still in it, and several boxes of broken glass, compact discs and dvds. A mattress was moved from the spare bedroom, and with a thorough vacuum of the rug some semblance of order returned to the now empty room. They unpacked the small amount of clothes and belongings David and his mother had managed to save when they moved to the Davidson's hotel.

After placing the hideous clown statue on the small table next to David's bed, they felt the room was once again inhabitable. Mrs. Whitman thanked Ben for all his help and asked him to stay for dinner. He gave his parent's a call and told Mrs. Whitman he'd be glad to stay. As she didn't know what food was still in the house, Mrs. Whitman asked them if they minded if she ran to grocery store and picked up some stuff first. They both said it was fine and the moment they could hear the sounds of her car leaving the driveway, Ben closed the door; he'd been waiting for hours to put his arms around David. It was obvious David was just as anxious for as soon as the door closed they were in each others arms and their lips were greedily kissing each other.

They stumbled to the bed and clumsily fell onto it. They shared a quick round of laughs before David pulled Ben on top of him and they continued their kisses. Since their first night in the cabin, they had been taking things slowly and had not done much experimenting, but as the intensity grew, Ben was growing more and anxious to go further. He pulled up for air and stared longingly into David's face; it was exactly as he always wanted to see him, happy, peaceful and full of joy.

"What are you thinking?"

"How beautiful you are . . ." Ben placed a gently kiss on his nose. "You are so handsome."

"Stop . . ." David laughed.

"No. You are perfect."

"I think you need glasses."

Ben didn't respond with words, instead he traced the line of David's shirt unbuttoning it as he went. He slid his hands inside and let his fingers play with the hair on David's chest. With his hands massaging David's chest, Ben kissed David's neck and playfully kissed his earlobe.

"I . . . I was thinking we might try something." He whispered into David's ear.

"Yeah? I was . . ." He sighed deeply. "I was thinking the same thing."

Ben sat up and met David's longing eyes. He loved David so much and he knew that David felt the same; they'd been telling each other it for weeks now. He'd never felt so strongly for someone before and for the first time in his life, he truly felt ready to take a relationship to the next level. He removed his hands from David's chest and slowly inched them to his belt buckle.

Nicholas

The old neighborhood looked remarkably the same. There were a few new stores in the strip mall near his parent's house and the burger joint had moved to the other side of the street but the houses, the trees, even the neighbors looked untouched by time. He hadn't been home in a year and even then that trip had been the first in a long time. It wasn't that he and his parent's didn't get along, in fact, they were the ones who were always traveling and visiting him. Driving down the main road he felt 16 again; he could even anticipate the flow of the traffic and the street lights; it was an odd sensation. He was pulled out of his reminiscing when he discovered he could no longer turn left onto his parent's street. Having to drive several blocks out of his way to turn around so he could turn right would have normally made him mad, but it didn't, he was glad to be home.

His parents, unfortunately, were not going to be home with him; they were out of town visiting his sister. He had the house to himself. Pulling into the driveway he noticed the house appeared more warmhearted than he remembered; the bushes he and his sister had brutalized as children were replaced with a wooden windmill, a fountain and a . . . Virgin Mary? Obviously a gift from his grandmother; he couldn't imagine his parents putting it there on their own.

He unloaded the car and dropped his bags in his old room. Gave the house a quick walk through to see what other differences his parents had made then was back in the car and on his way to visit Donna. He still hadn't been able to get her to agree to accompany him tonight, so this was his last ditch effort. When he first asked her she had responded sharply with a definite no. She said she never wanted to see that "stuck up, jack ass who treated Nic like a piece of shit" again. Nic knew better than to push the subject more so he waited a couple of days and asked again; she merely laughed. He was bound and determined to get her to agree today, he wanted to have at least one friend on his side; just in case.

He was sure that he would know many of the guests from either school or through passing during his time as Kevin's best friend, but what they knew of him and his life he could only guess. He had run into a few friends over the years and his sexual orientation seemed to be common knowledge, but the story of why he and Kevin weren't close anymore seemed to be the big question they all had. Some had believed that Nic and Kevin had something going on, while others heard odd stories ranging from fights with Carmen over Kevin to Nic forcing himself on Kevin. Nic's response was that they simply grew apart. However, everyone always commented on how much calmer and more at ease Nic seemed to be now. He thought so too, he was at a place in his life where being reminded of his past didn't make him uncomfortable; he was happy. He also made it a point to surround himself with friends and colleagues who were compassionate, outgoing, and happy.

Before he knew it he had arrived at the bookstore. He remembered his first trip here so many years ago; it was dark and scary. Now the store had been completely revamped; it was open, inviting, and warm, wooden bookcases had replaced the tacky old wire racks and big comfy looking lounge chairs replaced the old plastic lunch room style chairs. Classical music played softly through the store and numerous lighted candles added ambiance.

He noticed Donna talking animatedly with a young man with dark black hair; she had a book in one hand and by the way her other hand was wildly moving he knew she was talking it up. Nic waved to get her attention to no avail; she was too engrossed with the young man. He watched them talk and was amazed by how excited the two of them seemed to be about a book; the young man was as animated as Donna. They were joined by another young man, this one with brown hair, who placed an arm around the other man's shoulder and they instantly lent into each other. Nic was momentarily jealous; he knew the look shared between the two men well; new love. It had been quite some time since he had been close to anyone and he wished the two well. They only looked to be about eighteen or nineteen and love was so hard to maintain at that age.

Eventually Donna glanced his way and he waved again. She

noticed him this time and pointed him out to the boys who both smiled his way. He gave a wave unsure if he should join them or not; before he could make up his mind he noticed her excuse herself from the boys and she was running into his arms. She hugged him tightly.

"It's about time you got here! It's so good to see you."

"We see each other every month, except when you can't pull yourself away from Melissa."

"No! I mean here, at my store!"

"Oh, well it's not my fault you always come to me."

Donna released him and slugged his arm.

"It is your fault. This town is so boring we need any excuse to escape."

"Hey!" He rubbed his arm. "I bruise easily." He barely managed to say it without bursting into laughter.

"Damn! It is so good to see you here. So . . ." She spread out her arms to let him get a look around the store. "What do you think?"

Taking it all in, he had to say he was impressed. Before Donna and her partner Melissa had purchased the store he and Donna had come in as customers and had spent many an hour browsing; it was the first place they were able to be themselves. It rivaled a big chain store with its warmth and character now.

"You have done some remarkable work. The place looks even

more amazing in person. You're also still attracting the right crowd too."

He nodded towards the two boys Donna had been talking with.

"Enough of that." Donna said when she noticed who he was indicating. "Its very sweet actually; they are both in high school and have been friends for a very long time and just recently discovered their mutual attraction."

"Oh . . . really . . . I would have guessed they were older than that."

Donna seemed to recognize that Nic was reminded of his own situation with Kevin. She wrapped her arm in his and ushered him towards the back of the store.

"Yeah, Ben has been in here a couple of times, but this is his boyfriends first visit. Come on . . . let's go in the back and talk."

She glanced over her shoulder to the young man at the cash register.

"Kurt, I'll be in the back room with my friend. Holler if you need anything."

Kurt barely acknowledged Donna's announcement; she seemed to know that he heard her. She brought him to her office and he took a seat in the chair behind her desk while she sat on the corner of the desk. She lighted a cigarette and smiled as she saw the disgust on Nic's face, she knew he hated it.

"Isn't it illegal to smoke in here?"

"Yeah, but who is going to report me?"

"Okay, I'll give you that. I thought you were quitting?"

"I tried but work got to me again and I couldn't resist. Besides, it's my only vice. I don't drink, I don't do drugs, and I don't screw around."

"Don't look at me, I can't tell you the last time I went out and had a drink, except for the occasional beer with Christian. And as for sex . . . let's not go there."

"What? I don't get any stories of conquest from the college stud? Donna teased.

Nic eyed her with contempt. She knew that he was more the studying type than the party guy; he'd always been that way. Friends had assumed he and Donna were more rambunctious because of their outgoing attitudes, but in truth they were pretty bland. The most adventurous they had ever been was when they each got a tattoo on their legs and pierced their ears; Nic no longer wore his while Donna got many more.

"Oh you know I need to keep those escapades secret. I can't let it be known that I'm only passing by sleeping with the dean."

"Yeah right!" Donna rolled her eyes and took a deep drag on her cigarette. "Now, despite how happy I am to see you and talk with you, please tell me that there is some other reason for your visit aside from that God awful wedding?"

He didn't answer her; he spun in her chair, smiled meekly and tried to look as innocent as possible.

"Nic! Oh please . . . don't ask me."

"Come on, Donna. Please? Please, can't you imagine it?"

She rolled her eyes again and angrily stubbed her cigarette into the overflowing ashtray. She left her perch and sat in the chair across from her desk.

"I can imagine it and it makes me sick. Carmen will be in some hideous gown that will hardly look appealing on anyone and Kevin will be in some uppity tuxedo looking so smug and full of shit. Of course, then there will be that horrible bitch Jenny. God, where will they find enough fabric to make a dress for her? Nic, why do you want to put yourself through that?"

"I was invited."

"So what? I'm invited to my Aunt Jean's house every year for Christmas, but I know she doesn't really want me and Melissa there."

"That's different. I mean, Kevin did write that note saying . . ."

"Nic!" Donna interrupted. "Kevin wrote that note because he feels guilty. He treated you like shit and for some unknown reason he feels the need to continue punishing you."

It wasn't guilt, Nic was certain of that. He didn't know why he'd been invited but he preferred to imagine that Kevin and Carmen wanted him there to mend ties and clear the air. It didn't make sense if it was guilt.

"I think you're wrong. If it was a guilty conscience, why would he have included that message? They would have just sent a plain invitation."

"Maybe, but I can't help but feel that for some stupid reason Kevin wants to make you suffer. I mean, he must have known how you used to feel about him. It seems like he wants to make sure you know that you will never have him."

"Donna, seriously? My God, it's been almost two to three years since then."

"Think about it. Kevin knew you were gay and he used that to his advantage. He got what he wanted and then when he didn't need you anymore he threw you away like a piece of trash. And yes, you're right, it has been four years and now he's getting married and invites you out of the blue. What possible reason could he have; AND I don't buy the he wants to be friends argument. I'm sorry, but something doesn't seem right with this."

Nic couldn't believe Donna's argument, no matter how feasible it was. Okay, he did have to admit that maybe she was right in some small way. Could that be the feeling he still felt; did he lose all his sanity when it came to Kevin? No, he wasn't like that anymore.

"So you won't come with me?"

"Fine . . ." she relented. "Pick me up tonight at 5:00 pm . . . but remember you owe me big for this!"

He knew she was wrong about this. He knew that Kevin wasn't as sadistic as Donna suggested. He knew it.

Benjamin

The trip to the book store had been better than Ben could have hoped for; David loved it. He wanted to look at everything and found so many things that he wanted to buy; books, calendars, music, and t shirts. Ben had been saving his money for a few weeks and was able to purchase a couple of books and he was happy to know that he had managed to buy them without David realizing he'd actually bought them for him. They had also had a really good talk with Donna before her friend arrived. Ben had really connected with Donna on his previous trips and was glad that David had gotten to meet her too; they shared a love of humor so when she offered David some gay humor titles he seemed to devour them.

They spent longer than they anticipated at the store so their original plans for lunch were scrapped so that they could get home in time to meet James and Chuck who were coming over to do some gaming. They made it back to David's house with just enough time to scarf down some sandwiches, put their purchases away, and a quick make out session before the door bell rang.

"Dude, what the fuck took you so long to answer the door!" James announced. "Chuck thought you weren't home for a minute, but I knew that was Ben's dad's car in the drive."

"Come on in guys. Ben and I just finished lunch and I was cleaning the kitchen up or my mom would have had a fit." David fibbed.

"Okay, so I know you were all ready for a round of *Call of Duty* but look what I picked up today." James held up a copy of a new game they had all been dying to play for weeks now. "I'm ready to kick your asses."

"I don't know about that, David and I have been doing a lot of practicing lately. We might just give you a fighting chance today." Ben announced proudly. While it was true he and David had been playing a lot lately, most of their games were abandoned as they couldn't seem to concentrate on the game as they were too interested in playing with each other.

Chuck laughed. "I don't think it will matter, Ben. James always seems to beat us."

"I think Chuck has a point Ben." David said in agreement.

Their afternoon was quickly filled with laughter, jokes, profanity (mostly from James), and round after round of gaming as James continued to dominate the group with his winning streak. When it seemed like Ben was finally going to win one game, James announced he needed to leave soon. As the three stopped for a moment to look at him he managed a quick return with his controller and won the game.

"You cheated!" They all yelled.

"No. I really do need to split; I have to pick up Stephanie by 6:00. I can't help it if you all stopped playing."

Ben, David and Chuck abandoned their controllers. "We give up."

"Good choice, boys!" James said with delight.

"Screw you!" David sighed.

The guys quickly packed up the games and after some talk about school, James and Chuck left. Ben and David had enjoyed spending the afternoon with their friends; they hadn't had much time in the past couple of weeks since David had been doing so much with his parent's situation. But as much as they enjoyed the time with their friends, they were also looking forward to their first real dinner date. They'd had many a meal together since the night at the cabin, but this was their first dress up dinner.

They choose their favorite Italian restaurant and were fortunate to have been given a secluded booth and they took full advantage of being able to hold hands and talk openly. Their waiter noticed their hands and for the rest of the night gave them the best service they had ever had. He'd even offered to give them a free dessert to share. They declined but tipped heavily.

"I'm going to hit the restroom before we leave." Ben said.

"Sure, I'll be out in the waiting area."

Ben was adjusting his coat as he exited the restroom and wasn't looking where he was going and bumped into several people. He started to apologize but his words caught in his throat as he discovered he had humped into Karen.

"Benjamin?"

"Um . . . Karen . . . I didn't, I didn't see you there." He stammered.

Karen looked him over and seemed to notice how nicely he was dressed. She met his stare and he could have sworn that she looked upset.

"What brings you to this restaurant, Benji? Are . . . are you, like, here on a date?"

"What? A . . . a date?" He wanted to say yes so desperately but knew now was not the time or the place. "No, no . . . David and I . . . David and I are just out um . . . celebrating."

She suddenly became excited.

"Oh really? What are you celebrating? Did one of you get, like, the national honor society award? I heard that they were, like, announcing them this week. Oh My God! That would be so, like, totally awesome if one of you go it."

Shit! What the hell was he going to tell her? Maybe she would just keep talking and he wouldn't have to come up with an answer. He watched as she continued to rattle on and on. Then, he noticed she seemed to be winding down. Damn, please, please, please do not let her ask again, he prayed.

"So what is it that you're celebrating?"

Oh crap! He opened his mouth and before he could say a word he heard David's voice.

"Karen! What a surprise." He came up to Ben and placed an arm around his shoulder. "I guess Ben here told you that I got accepted to U of M, right? I was so happy I told him we just had to celebrate tonight."

Ben sighed with relief. Thank goodness David must have heard part of what Karen had been saying and had been able to come up with an excuse.

"Way to go, David. That is, like, awesome."

"Yeah, I know. Well . . . we have to run." David said quickly not giving Karen a chance to interject. "Ben and I have to get home soon; we promised his mom we'd watch his brother tonight. Bye."

Ben nodded an agreement and they left the restaurant. Once they were safely inside the car, they burst out in laughter.

"Holy Shit! What are the freakin' odd that she would be there?"

"Ben, you are so lucky you are gay because your taste in girls sucks!"

As Ben backed the car out of the parking spot and began to drive out of the restaurant he checked his rear-view mirror and could see Karen standing in the door watching them leave. His hand sought out David's and grasped it tightly.

Nicholas

The wedding had not been as lavish or over the top as Nic imagined it would be. The church had been decorated with white lace and silk with small touches of silver and red. It was gorgeous and peaceful, almost Martha Stewart-esque; not at all what he would have expected. The only real surprise was that it was a full Catholic service. He knew Kevin, like himself, had been raised in the Catholic Church, but during their entire friendship Kevin professed the Catholic beliefs as a farce. He could only guess that Kevin either reverted back to Catholicism or was going along with it for Carmen and her family. Donna hated every second of, but decided she was going to accept the Communion as a protest; she returned to their pew with the wafer still in hand. She squeezed the paper thin wafer until it crumbled into dust.

When the service ended Nic and Donna fought the urge to run and hide instead of waiting through the receiving line, no matter how much he hated the idea of introducing himself to people he would never see or talk to again, he wanted to see Kevin and Carmen. Moving through the line he noticed Jenny, she hadn't seen him yet; she was smiling and laughing with someone. After a moment she looked his way and did a double take; her smile disappeared as she realized it was him. He continued to smile for a moment and then looked away; he didn't care, he wasn't here to see her. The closer he got to Jenny the more he could see her fidget. When he was three people away she began to sneeze and excused herself from the line. Donna nudged his side and whispered into his ear. "What a bitch." He couldn't help but laugh.

Kevin's parent's heard him and pulled him into a hug. They told him how happy they were to see him. He left them and met Carmen's smiling face that immediately became more animated as she threw her arms around his neck and kissed his cheeks.

"Oh my God, Nic! I am so happy that you came. Oh, how I've missed you."

"Congratulations, Carmen. I'm very happy for you and Kevin. I can't believe you guys were able to wait this long."

She kissed his cheek again. "Tell me about it. Oh, Nic! I can't tell you how wonderful it is to see you. You better be saving a dance for me later."

"Of course."

Carmen obviously wanted to talk more, but they were holding up the line. She hugged him again and told him they would catch up later. As Carmen turned to Donna Nic shuffled a few steps and the moment he had been waiting for was upon him. His heart raced and he took a quick breath and met Kevin's eyes. His smile was as bright and animated as Carmen's.

His eyes widened with excitement and gave Nic a once over as if he was making sure it truly was Nic. Nic put out his hand, Kevin accepted it and pulled Nic into a brotherly hug.

"It is so good to see you Nic. I wasn't, I wasn't sure if you were going to come or not."

"I wouldn't have missed it."

"You have truly made this day perfect for us."

Nic felt a wave of warmness come over him. He had not expected such kind and heartwarming greetings. Kevin smiled again and then noticed Donna next to Nic.

"Donna? Wow, you look great. Thank you for coming."

"Thanks . . .um . . . congratulations." Donna fumbled for words.

Kevin returned his attention to Nic.

"Look Nic, I'm really glad you are here. Let's have a drink later and talk."

"That would be great."

He didn't want to but Nic let Donna move them into the reception hall just off the church. They found their assigned table, amazingly close to the head table.

"See, Donna, I told you it would be okay."

"The night is still young. I'll wait till it is over before passing judgment."

"I can't believe you had the gall to show up!"

The hair on the back of his neck stood on edge; the change in the air was instantaneous, almost as if there had been a current of electricity in the room. There was no denying the disgust and hatred in Jenny's deep voice. She had purposely avoided looking at him throughout dinner and she seemed to disappear for the first portion of the reception. Now that the dancing and partying was in full swing however, here she was.

Nic had gone to the bar to get a drink and when he turned back towards the party her massive figure was before him. She had her arms wrapped across her chest and she appeared to be scowling at him. He knew she was trying to appear frightening but just as it had been in high school, her massive figure and heavily made up face made her look sad and almost clown-like.

"Jenny. It is a . . . um . . . it's you." He purposely fumbled over the fake greeting. He knew he shouldn't be so petty with her, but he wasn't about to let her intimidate him.

She inched closer to him.

"What the fuck are you doing here?"

"I'm getting a drink."

"That doesn't answer my question."

"Then ask me a question that isn't so redundant. Surely, even you can ask me a simple question, right?"

It took her a minute or two to realize what he was asking and for her to formulate a new question.

"Why did you come to this wedding?"

"I was invited."

"You are not welcome or wanted here. Didn't we make that clear years ago?"

"I came here because Kevin and Car . . ."

"I knew IT!" She spat out. Her scowl disappeared and was replaced by a bizarre smile. "You sick, son of a bitch. I can't believe it."

"What are you babbling about?"

"You're still in love with Kevin!"

Nic laughed out loud. "In love with Kevin? Oh that's a good one, Jenny. I think you need your head examined."

"Don't even try to deny it. I knew you were a fag the moment I met you and I knew that you were after Kevin. Carmen used to tell me I was imagining it, but I saw the way you looked at him. It gave you away every time. And it's obviously still there."

"I'm sorry to disappoint you, but you couldn't be further from the truth."

"Don't mess with me fag-boy." She inched closer again. "They were your friends and they were thankfully smart enough to realize what you were really after. You wanted to destroy their love with your sick . . ."

"Fuck off, Jenny!" Nic wasn't about to listen to any more of her nonsense. He started to push past her but Jenny's arm whipped out incredibly fast for its size and latched onto his arm. It took a few pulls, but he managed to pull it from her grasp.

"What the hell are you doing? I don't know what you think you know or what you think you saw and I don't care. I came here today because I was invited by my friends." This time he inched closer to her. "So get the hell out of my face and leave me alone."

"You don't scare me fag-boy. I know what I saw. Carmen and Kevin love each other very, very much. I will not allow you to hurt them."

"Whatever." Nic attempted to leave again, but she blocked his way.

"You are not welcome here. So go pick up the dyke date and get your little fag ass out of here before I throw you out."

Nic stood his ground and cracked a smile. He couldn't believe she though she scared him.

"I told you to get the fuck out of here!"

"Jenny!"

Jenny's face flushed red with fear and embarrassment. She forced a smile to her face, turned to find Kevin behind her. "Kevin?" Her voice was high pitched and full of phony happiness. "I didn't hear you come up . . . are you having a good time? You know, it's almost time for you and Carmen to cut the cake."

Kevin sighed; he pulled his glasses from his nose and rubbed his brow. Nic hadn't noticed him approach either, but from the tone of his voice he was positive that Kevin had heard at least some of Jenny's and his confrontation. He knew Kevin was angry and was attempting to tame it.

"Jenny." He said tightly. "Nic is our guest tonight; mine and Carmen's! He is to be treated with respect. I'm sure he did not come here tonight to be berated with innuendo from high school. We've all grown up a lot since then and I would appreciate it if you would let go of those old thoughts and feelings."

"Oh Kevin, you are so right." She hugged him and whispered apologies to him in her sweetest voice. "I just feel so protective of you and Carmen. I guess . . . I guess I let that control me."

"Sorry Nic." She uttered with complete disgust and a look that Nic could only imagine meant she wished him dead. She smiled to Kevin and rejoined the rest of the party.

The surge of energy flowing through him was more than Nic had expected; he couldn't believe he had let her get him so worked up. He downed his drink in one quick swig. As he felt himself calm, he felt almost defeated; he didn't want Kevin to think he couldn't handle what Jenny was saying to him.

"Thanks. You didn't have to do that. I could have handled her."

"I know. You always could; one of the few who could." Kevin returned his glasses to nose and placed a hand on Nic's shoulder. "Let me get you a new drink."

"That's not necessary . . ."

"I know, but it will give us a chance to talk."

Kevin ushered Nic back to bar and ordered them both a drink. He handed Nic the glass and offered a toast. "To . . . new beginnings."

"New beginnings and congratulations." Nic added.

As they drank Nic noticed that Kevin's eyes never left his. It was odd and comforting both at the same time. It was if Kevin was looking for something.

"What is it?" Nic asked.

"I . . . I meant the toast to be for us; you and me; a new beginning to our friendship. I'm truly glad you came tonight. I've thought of you a lot these past couple of years; I know I can't make up for all the hurt I caused you. I hope we can move beyond what happened. I do want us to be friends again. I've missed you."

It was what Nic had longed to hear Kevin say; he was genuinely sorry for what transpired between them. As happy as he was though he couldn't easily forget Jenny's words; for she had been right about one thing,

Nic had been in love with Kevin once, but those feelings died a long time ago. If Jenny had somehow truly noticed his feelings he was sure that she had told Carmen her suspicions as well.

"Thank you. I'd, I'd like that too. It's . . . It's just . . . well . . ."

"You're not worried about Jenny are you?"

"No. Definitely not her." Nic laughed. "No, I think my concern is Carmen. I know that she is happy to see me today, but what about tomorrow. I'd be a fool not to believe that Jenny hasn't shared her . . . let's call it, dislike of me with her."

Kevin placed a hand on Nic's arm guiding him from the bar to a small table nearby.

"Nicky." Kevin's voice lowered.

Nicky. He had once loved the nickname. Growing up he had always been called Nic or Nicholas but from the moment they became friends Kevin called him Nicky. No one else could get away with it like Kevin could; there was just something about the way it rolled off his tongue. Once on a date a potential boyfriend had called him it and his stomached soured. Now, however, it was old and familiar and sounded perfect.

"Carmen doesn't know anything about what happened between us. That will always stay between you and me. When Jenny started attacking you, it was me that chose to pull away. I was too scared that she would accuse me or worse, guess what happened. Carmen didn't want to pull away; she was very upset that we did."

Kevin took a drink and continued. "About two years ago Carmen was going through old photos and came across some of the three of us. We got to talking and she asked me what happened between us. She wanted to know why I pulled away."

"What did you tell her?"

"I told her that you had shared the news of your life style choice . . ."

"It's not a choice." Nic interjected defensively and then regretted it. He was so used to having to say that to people that sometimes it came out before he even knew he was saying it. "Sorry about that. It's a force of habit."

"No you are right. I shouldn't have said it like that, sorry. Where . . . oh yeah, so I told Carmen that you had confided in me and that I was having some difficulty dealing with it. She told me that I had been stupid. She even accused me of letting Jenny influence me."

They shared a laugh.

"I am truly sorry, Nicky. I was young, stupid and a jerk. I'm sorry I wasn't a better friend."

This evening was like a dream; all the things he had ever wanted to hear were being said to him tonight. In all his imaginings of this event, he often saw himself telling Kevin how much he hurt him, telling him to fuck off, or even asking him why he wasn't a better friend; this was what he'd been hoping for. He was relieved to know that he no longer felt the anger and frustration he once had.

"I don't know if this is the right time or place . . . oh what the hell. It took me a long time to get over what happened between us. There was even a time that I thought I never would. I don't regret what happened, but I remember a time when I wished it hadn't. However, I know I wouldn't be the person I am today had it not. I do forgive you; in fact I need to thank you."

Kevin sat flabbergasted. "Thank me? Nicky? I was a shit to you."

"I know that, but it took me a long time to realize that our situation actually helped me. It forced me to grow up and see the world with new eyes, new expectations, and realize that I control my own destiny. I'm not that little boy who blindly follows and does what people expect me to do. I do what I want, when I want and I don't worry about what people think. I know what it truly means to love someone and to love myself."

Kevin smiled. "I'm so glad for you Nicky."

Nic smiled.

"So another toast." Kevin raised his glass. "To my friend, who I am anxious to get to know again."

Benjamin

Once again talk of getting tattoos has arisen. It has been the hot topic for more than a week now. I think Sarah, David and I have been talking about nothing else. Why? Because James sneaked out and got one; when I say sneaked out I mean he has yet to tell his parents about it, even though he is 18. I have to admit I was amazed at how decent a tattoo it is too. I know how over the top James can be sometimes so when he first told me he got one I expected his entire arm to be covered in something hideous. It's quite tame for him; he got a Celtic design arm band. It was incredibly detailed and not something I would have thought he would ever choose. However the moment I asked him what possessed him to get such a design he replied in his normal out going manner that it looked "fucking awesome". He said it took several hours to do and hurt like hell (obviously I am not being as colorful as James in his description).

The three musketeers have been trying to figure out what we would do and it is not as easy as I thought it would be. We checked out a bunch of books from the library and checked some tattoo websites but everything is so varied; and despite how close we are the three of us all wants something vastly different. Sarah wants a flower, but not just any flower mind you, she

wants a violet - the first flower Christian ever gave her - and she wants it

on her calf. David wants something on his shoulder blade like Christian -

he has the word peace in Kanji. When Sarah was here David said was

leaning more towards a musical note or possible a line from his favorite

song. After Sarah left and it was just the two of us, he told me that he really

wants a pink triangle with my initials in it. I love him so much!

As for me, I wasn't able to narrow it down so easily. I've had so many

thoughts and ideas about what I might possibly want to do some day but it

wasn't until last night when David told me about the pink triangle that I

realized what I'd want. And yes, while David's initials are a fantastic idea

too and who knows it might have to be my second one, but if I do decide to

get a tattoo I want my first one to be a bit more personal. I want David's

signature on the inside of my wrist. When I was going through one of the

websites I noticed that Robbie Williams has one with his grandfather's

name. I can't say why I want it there as I can only imagine how painful it

would be, but something about it seems right. I know it sounds crazy, I

mean how can I possibly think of doing something so permanent with the

first person I have ever loved. But this is different, this isn't some

ordinary crush between high school students, I know that. David and I have

been friends for so long we connect on a level far deeper than even I thought was possible. He truly is the love of my life and I could not imagine what I would do without him. He has helped me in so many ways. Perhaps that is the secret of life long . . .

"Benjamin?"

He looked up from his journal to find his mother standing in the door way; she was wrapped in her robe and looking sleepy.

"Yeah . . .?"

His mom took a few steps inside and sat in the chair next to his bed. She pointed to the clock which read 3:07 am. Ben couldn't believe he'd been writing for almost two hours.

"I know that you don't have a set bedtime anymore and you don't have school tomorrow, but it is awfully late. Are you planning on staying up all night?"

He smiled sheepishly; it had not been his intention to be up so late. He had simply wanted to jot some thoughts down and ended up becoming engrossed. "Sorry mom. I didn't realize the time."

"What are you writing, if you don't mind me asking?"

"No, nothing really important. I'm writing down my thoughts and feelings, the day's events, stuff that happened at school or with friends. Things like that."

"You've really taken to that journal, I'm so glad. Who knows, perhaps you have the next great American novel inside you."

"You never know."

"I won't keep you; I'm heading back to bed. Please don't stay up too late, you do have to work in the afternoon and then dinner with the gang."

"I won't. I'm almost done."

His mother rose from the chair, bent forward and kissed his forehead. "Good night, Ben."

Ben returned to his journal and finished his thought. He capped the pen, closed the journal and fastened the leather strap. He opened the drawer of his night stand and returned the journal to its normal spot. He did want to make sure he got some sleep; he was looking forward to dinner as Christian was in town and would be joining them. Plus, Christian was also bringing his room mate Nic along and Sarah couldn't wait for the guys to meet him. Tattoos aside, it was all she talked about this week. It was going to be a great night.

Sarah

Sarah bounced down the steps of the staircase delighted that morning had finally arrived; Christian was coming home and she couldn't wait to see him. He'd been so busy with his final projects for school that he'd had to cancel their last two planned weekends. Before they knew it a month had passed without them seeing each other and they were both pretty anxious to get together. She was so excited that she spent most of the night tossing and turning instead of sleeping.

Sarah hurried through the lobby and went directly to the family's private kitchen / breakfast nook. Her parents were already seated and eating; they noticed their daughter and gasped. It wasn't often that Sarah joined them for breakfast on a weekend; most times she was already out with the guys or still sleeping.

"Good morning darling. To what do we owe the pleasure of your company on such a beautiful morning? Let me guess, you and the boys are heading out soon or you've finally decided that sleeping away your weekends wasn't a good use of time?"

She kissed her father's cheek and faked a laugh at his joke.

"Very funny, daddy."

Her mother rose from the table and filled a plate with eggs, hash browns and toast. She placed it in front of her daughter and gently touched her shoulder.

"I think I can guess what brought her out so early today?"

Her father's eyes opened wide with question. "What would that be?"

Sarah's cell phone rang before she could answer.

"I know . . . I know . . . no calls at the table, but it's Christian. He's on his way home today. I promise it will be quick."

She answered before her parents could protest.

"Hi you . . . what?"

Her mother looked at her father and smiled. "There's your answer."

"I should have guessed. He's the only other person besides Ben or David that could get her to do anything."

"Daddy!" She pulled the phone from her ear and offered a phony expression of hurt. When she saw him smile and return to eating, she returned the phone to her ear.

"Sorry about that, my father is being quite the joker today. Yes . . . yes . . . oh really? Oh I am so glad. Of course I'm sure they will get along. Of course. Look, Christian, I have to go. I'll see you in a little while. Bye."

She flipped her phone shut and smiled at her father.

"See . . . it was just a quick call."

After breakfast with her parents, Sarah returned to her room to finish getting ready. She wanted to look extra nice today, not only for Christian, but for Nic too. When Christian had first suggested that Nic meet the guys, she couldn't believe she hadn't thought of it before and she had wanted it that night, but unfortunately that wasn't possible. Then with Christian's project taking up so much of his time it had been so hard for her not to become anxious. She had adored Nic from almost the moment she first meet him and she just knew that the guys would like him. The question was how to let the guys know that Nic was gay; she couldn't remember if they knew it or not. She was sure she had probably mentioned it before, but it was probably something that hadn't really stuck before. There had to be some way to let me know. She hoped that once they saw how much she and Christian supported Nic that they would find the comfort to admit it as well.

If all else failed, maybe Nic and the guys would at least become friends; they were bound to like him. At the very least she hoped that perhaps Ben and David would find Nic to be someone they could at least ask questions to. They needed some gay friends, unless of course they already had some, she wondered. No, besides herself the only other friends they hung out with were James and Chuck and Sarah knew definitely that neither of them was gay. Stephanie tended to share a lot with Sarah about her and James sex life and as for Chuck, Sarah and him dated briefly eons ago. He was quiet but definitely not gay.

Tonight would be a new beginning for them, she was sure of it. Graduation was just over a month away, prom was around the corner, and their lives were inching towards adulthood. Tonight would be filled with talk of the future and their plans for it. This was going to be beginning of their new lives and she couldn't wait.

Benjamin

Saturday -

The past couple of days have been pretty busy but two big events did take place and both sorta have to do with David and me coming out. Its odd because my past few journal entries have been filled with my own thoughts and questions about whether or not we should tell Sarah or family; it was almost as if I knew that this would be the weekend . . . okay . . . I'm getting ahead of myself. So let's start with Thursday . . .

David had another round of pranks calls from his father that night. Even though they had the numbers changed at the house, somehow the jerk was able to get them. I was spending the night since we didn't have school on Friday and the phone must have rang at least twelve times. His mom phoned the police and they were able to track his father down and the calls stopped, but at the same time both David and I learned that his father had been sending his mom clippings with bible quotes and other anti-gay messages lately. Mrs. Whitman didn't tell David about them because she didn't want him to worry, but since she'd been turning them over to the police and as the calls were something new they brought it up in front of us.

I was very proud of David though, he didn't show any emotion or discomfort in front of the police he just let them talk and the moment they left he told his mom that he understood why she didn't tell him. He then asked if she wouldn't hide things like this from him. I had tried to excuse myself, but David asked me to stay and I was glad I did. It was so nice to see him and his mom talking so openly about things. Once we were back in his room I told him I how proud I was. He kissed me and told me that he didn't want to hide anything from his mom because they needed to support one another through this.

Then Friday morning while his mom was making us breakfast she came right out and asked us if we were dating. I nearly spit out my cereal but David, very matter of fact replied that yes, we were . He asked her if that was problem, and I have to give Mrs. Whitman a lot of credit, she said no. She said she thought something changed between us recently. It was so amazing. She sat down with us and talked about being careful and being good to each other and stuff. She asked us lots and lots of questions too and we did our best to answer them. Again, I have to give Mrs. Whitman a lot of credit; I highly doubt my parents or many parents for that matter would have been as matter of fact about things. Nothing seemed to faze her either.

As I said it was awesome, but also a little nerve racking as well. It took me a while to get comfortable with it, but once David took my hand in his and his mother told us she loved us both, all my fears disappeared. Being able to sit in his house watching a movie and being able to hold hands and put my head on his shoulder without worry was great.

That takes me to last night . . . our dinner with Christian, Sarah and Nic. Sarah had been talking about Nic for years now, but we had never had the chance to meet before, so when she told us he was coming we were looking forward to finally putting a face to the name. However, the moment we saw him we both panicked - he was Donna's friend from the bookstore. I thought our secret was out. When I think about it now I realize that it sounds odd that we were scared about telling our best friends when we'd just come out to David's mom, but we still weren't sure we were ready to share our secret yet.

It was obvious that Nic recognized us as well. When Sarah made the introductions, he shook each of our hands and gave us a little wink. He told us it was nice to finally meet us as he'd heard so much about us from Christian and Sarah. I wondered if our secret was safe. Then as if by chance another friend of Christian's was in the restaurant so he and Sarah went over to say Hi. The moment we were alone with Nic he told us not worry as he knew that we were not out to Christian and Sarah yet. I think I

started to ramble some sort of thank you. He told us he understood, but that

when we were ready, Christian and Sarah would support us. Though I

think we both assumed the answer, David asked him how he knew and Nic

replied that they supported him being gay.

Once Sarah and Christian returned the most amazing conversation took

place. The five of us talked almost non-stop; it was if Nic was always part

of our group. We talked about so many plans ands dreams for after

graduation. We've had conversations like this before, however this time it

was deeper. Long gone were the old talks of what we were thinking of

doing, our conversations were real. I'm not doing our conversation justice,

but to say it was fantastic doesn't cut it either. It was amazing. For the first

time I feel like an adult.

David and I excused ourselves after dinner and went to the bathroom and

had a quick conversation. After the level of sharing and emotions we'd

been having we knew we couldn't hide it any longer. We went back to the

table and told them we had an announcement. Before David could even

finish that both he and I were gay and were dating Sarah was out of her

chair and hugging the both of us. Christian and Nic were soon

congratulating us as well. We dominated the conversation for the next hour as Sarah grilled us with question after question. I have to give Christian credit; he truly is the coolest straight guy I've ever met. I was worried he'd be uncomfortable with the turn of the conversation, but he wasn't.

Another plus to this already great dinner was that Christian brought along his camera and took lots and lots of pictures; there is one of David and I that can not wait to get a copy of - we're both smiling so brightly and it is our first photo as an out couple.

In just a short time we came out to David's mom and our dearest friends. Plus we also made a new friend. Nic was wonderful. When we left he gave us his phone number and email address and told us if we ever needed to talk to contact him. He also told us how happy he was to have met us and was looking forward to getting to know us better. We told him we agreed.

All in all - a great, amazing, and awesome weekend.

Till next time . . .

B -

Sarah

Sarah swept through the crowd of students waving hello to friends and smiling at boys who adored her from afar. Her locker was surrounded by people but what surprised her most was that James and Stephanie were using it as a support for their aggressive make out session. It took a few clearings of her throat for the two of them to disengage their lips and actually notice she was there.

"Oh . . . hey. Sorry about that Sarah, Steph and I didn't notice you there."

"Obviously, but then how could my friend have seen me with the way you were attacking her lips."

"You're in early . . . that is good."

"I had some things to do this morning." She had gotten up early to send Christian and Nic on their way back to school. "So can you let my friend go so I can get in my locker, please?"

"Of course he can, right James?" Stephanie untangled herself from James' arms. "So did you have a good visit with Christian?"

"It was so good, Stephanie." Her dislike of James disappeared as she shared girl talk. "We had dinner with the guys on Saturday and then got to spend all of yesterday out doing some hiking in the fields. Christian also got some fantastic photos done while we were out too. Then we had a romantic dinner for two at our favorite restaurant last night. We sat for hours talking. It was fantastic."

"Oh, I am so glad. I know you were so looking forward to seeing him."

James sighed loudly and lent against the locker next to hers. He rolled his eyes at the girl talk and stared anxiously at Sarah.

"Oh no, what do you want James? Did you forget about the government assignment again?"

James smiled and for once Sarah knew he wasn't hitting her up for homework help. If it wasn't homework, she thought, what on earth could it be?

"No, no, no." Stephanie said proudly. "He did his homework. I made sure of that last night."

"Good for you."

"I know. Actually, James thought you might be interested in some . . . well . . . let's call it some news I heard."

"Wait a minute; I must be hearing things incorrectly. Does James Ingram want to tell me some gossip?"

James shrugged his shoulders and without saying a word Sarah knew that it was true. She could tell that he wanted her to ask him, so she deliberately took her time going through the items in the locker. She could see he was squirming.

"Oh come on! Shit. I know you well enough to know that you will want to hear this. Cut the fucking bullshit and let me tell you."

Sarah giggled. "Oh alright. What is it?"

James became overly excited and it surprised Sarah. She had never seen him like this.

"Yesterday Stephanie was told that Ben has a date to the prom. Now, I know that for a fact he is going stag; he told me himself. Yet, this person says he isn't and he is definitely taking someone."

Sarah was stunned; could James and Stephanie somehow discovered the secret she had just been told. Did they know Ben and David were a couple? No, it couldn't be that. They had told Sarah that no one except for David's mom knew. Had someone at school seen them somewhere or something? No, she was jumping to conclusions and she had to stop. James had not given any indication for her to think his conversation was going towards the truth. His jovial excitement was for some other reason.

"Oh and who is this mystery person?" She asked.

"Prepare yourself . . . you ready?"

"James! Tell me."

"Karen Wright."

"What?" Her relief washed over her and was then replaced by shock and then absurdity. Psycho Karen? Someone actually thought that Ben was taking her to the prom?

James and Stephanie were laughing almost as hard as Sarah. James steadied himself and continued. "Are you ready for the kicker?"

"Oh my . . . there can't be more, please tell me there isn't more?"

"There is." Stephanie said. "The person, who told me, was Karen herself. She came right up to me at the mall yesterday. I didn't even notice she was talking to me at first, but then she's asking me about prom and then she shows me this dress she bought and told me that Ben was taking her. At first, it didn't register so I said "Ben who". She looks at me and says "Like, Ben Tolliver of course!", can you believe it?"

"Oh . . . my . . . God; you're kidding me, right? This is a joke?"

"I swear we're serious." James raised his hand as if taking an oath. "She told Stephanie that they even booked a hotel room for some celebrating afterward; if you get my drift."

Sarah was laughing but at the same time her mind was racing with ideas. She couldn't wait to tell the guys, but her first priority was to find Karen and see if it was true. She couldn't believe that Karen was so desperate to lie to people. Then it hit her, she and Karen shared homeroom together. A plan suddenly appeared in her mind.

"Thanks for the scoop, you two. I owe you. I've got an idea and I need to split. See you later."

"I know that look. I just wish I could be there to see what it is you're doing."

"I'll tell you both later."

Sarah didn't wait for them to answer she had to get to homeroom. She tended to be right on time or a minute past the bell, but today she made it in record time. Karen was already at a seat, book open and pen scribbling away as she talked with another classmate that Sarah didn't recognize, then again she didn't really know half the people in homeroom since it was simply a place for attendance to be taken and announcements to be shared.

Sarah kept a watchful eye on Karen as she made her way around the room. Karen and the girl were so involved with their talk that they didn't even notice when Sarah took the seat immediately behind them. She listened in on the discussion the two were having and ignored the noise of the other students filing into the room. She could hear the other girl saying something about graduation and Karen telling her that she was going away to school. Damn, why isn't she telling the girl about her big date to prom? She thought her plan would backfire until she heard the other girl saying how lucky Karen was to have such a great boyfriend who was willing to chance colleges so they could be together.

Sarah forced herself not to laugh out loud as she heard Karen saying how sweet her "man" was. She pulled her cell from her pocket and raised the volume of her ringer. She pressed the button and her phone sounded, loudly. Sarah pretended to be surprised and mouthed an apology as she answered the phony call.

"Hello?" She sang out much louder than she would ever answer the phone. It had the effect she was hoping for as Karen turned around and looked at her. Karen looked her over and rolled her eyes.

"Oh hi Ben, what's the emergency, homeroom is just about to start?" Sarah stared directly at Karen as she saw the anger in her eyes disappear, replaced with a look Sarah could only guess was fear.

"What? You are kidding, I didn't hear that. Someone is telling everyone that you are taking *WHO* to the prom?"

The color drained from Karen's face and her mouth dropped

open.

"Seriously Ben. Who would ever believe that you would take her to prom. Everyone knows that you . . . DO. NOT. LIKE. HER!" Sarah punctuated the last words.

The girl who sat in front of Karen looked back and forth from Sarah to Karen and then turned around.

Karen's face filled with angry tears. She opened her mouth just as the bell rang.

"Oops, got to go!" Sarah snapped the phone shut. Her overly cheerful facade faded and she lowered her voice. "Was there something you wanted to say Karen?"

Ms. Kenny entered the room and called the class to order before Karen could say a word. Karen turned slowly back to the front of the class; she didn't utter a word or look at another person during the entire 15 minutes of homeroom. When the bell rang she scattered into the halls.

Sarah sat back in her seat, she knew that what she had done wasn't the nicest thing and Christian would probably lecture her about it, but she had to defend Ben. She didn't like that Karen was spreading false rumors about him and she wouldn't stand for it. She did what any friend would have done.

Christian

He removed the slides from the light box placing an X on those he knew wouldn't work. He added the next set of slides to box and began critiquing them. He had narrowed the pile of pictures down to ten and was now trying to narrow those ten down to three. If this was a normal project the process would take several days of deliberation and consultation with his advisers, however this wasn't a project for school, it was personal. He'd been trying to figure out what type of gift he wanted to get Sarah, David and Ben for their prom/graduation and after their recent dinner a couple of weeks ago and the hundreds of photos he had taken that night he knew what he wanted to get them; a picture of the group that captured their unique bond of love, friendship and support. It was a daunting task but he wanted them to know how honored he felt to be included in their lives. If that meant he had to work on it in his free time and without the use of the computers in the photo lab so be it; the looks on their faces would be worth it.

He examined the slides again and managed to eliminate another four. The remaining six photos each had all the aspects that he thought brought out the personalities of the group; the problem was attempting to find something minuscule in the photo that bothered him enough to eliminate it. He checked his watch and wished Nic was home; he was good about offering advice on his work. Especially after meeting the guys and now talking on the phone, emailing, or Facebooking them, he could offer some new insight.

Christian slunk in his chair and sighed. He could only guess that Nic would not be home for some hours yet, he was out with Kevin and Carmen. Ever since Nic had gone to their wedding he'd heard from them at least once a week; tonight though was their second visit. They had invited Christian to join them but he knew he would never get any work done if he had. He had to give Nic credit though, he didn't know if he could have forgiven Kevin so easily; especially with the circumstances of why they stopped talking. Christian liked to think of himself as a generally level headed person who tried to find the best in everyone, but he knew first hand what a sore spot Kevin had been to Nic. He'd been surprised and happy when Nic told him about the talk he had with Kevin at the wedding and since; it did seem like Kevin truly did regret everything and after meeting them tonight he had to admit that he found them pleasant and very friendly.

Christian was also the first to notice that Nic seemed so much happier lately, though he believed it had more to do with meeting Ben and David than anything else.

Christian switched off the light table, vowing to work with the pictures on the computer tomorrow. He logged into his laptop and checked his email. He had his standard barrage of emails from Sarah; most were no more than a sentence or two so they were easy to get through quickly. He checked some blogs, the news, and a few other sites before logging off. He turned on the TV and found an episode of Family Guy on so he thought he'd veg out before turning in.

He got half way through the episode before the phone rang. He picked up and answered.

"Hey Christian, how's it going?"

"Ben. What's up?"

"Not too much, though I am sure Sarah would have already filled you in on anything if there was."

"Very true. So what can I do for you, man?"

"I was wondering if Nic was around. I had a question for him."

"Sorry, but he went out with some friends. I'm not sure when he'll be back.

"Oh." Ben sounded disappointed.

"Is there anything I can help with?" Christian offered. He knew that the guys had been asking Nic's advice on how to come out to Ben's parents but he thought they had decided not to cross that bridge yet. Was Ben still debating that?

"Um . . ."

"Is everything okay, Ben?"

"What? Oh yeah . . . its just . . . I had a question about . . . um . . . well its kinda . . . personal."

Personal? Christian heard the nervousness in Ben's voice and he almost laughed as he realized what Ben wanted to talk to Nic about.

"Sex. Right?"

"Oh . . . well, yeah." Ben laughed. "I don't know why I was so nervous saying it out loud. I think I'm still getting used to being able to talk openly about these things."

"I understand. So the expert isn't it, but might I be of some assistance? Now before you start thinking that you will gross or creep me out, don't worry. Sex is sex, gay or straight. Scarily, thanks to Nic, I know way more than any straight man should now about some things."

"You . . . you sure?"

"Ben, I wouldn't have offered if I wasn't. Who knows, I just might know the answer too."

"Okay . . . here goes . . ."

Nicholas

"Remember building the homecoming float? You and Kevin were so bored you tied trash bags around your heads and were jumping around like idiots?"

"Oh my gosh." Nic said mortified at the memory. "What were we thinking?"

"We were seniors, Nicky. We thought we ruled the world. We could do no wrong." Kevin said quoting the motto that almost every senior in their class seemed to say.

"Oh, if only we could go back to those innocent days." Carmen said dreamily and then looked at the guys and laughed. "No thank you."

Nic took a swig of his beer as the laughter continued across their table. Dinner had been finished long ago and now they were having far too much fun recalling the good old days. Carmen had started a class alumni website and brought along copies of newsletters and updates of former friends and classmates. She had even shared that several visitors to her site asked about Nic. They had so many fun, stupid, embarrassing, and crazy memories from their school days and they seemed to be sharing them all. At the same time they were catching up on the events that had taken place during their years apart.

Their lives had taken turns they had not expected, Carmen was still an Executive Assistant instead of an accountant; Nic was preparing to graduate next quarter with a degree in history instead of psychology and Kevin was working in an advertising agency instead of becoming a teacher but they still connected. Despite the changes and the time apart they still shared many of the same tastes. Nic had once believed that he would never be able to sit and talk with Kevin and Carmen like this again. He assumed the gap would never be bridged; he had moved on and made so many new friends. He was glad that he was wrong and he couldn't have asked for better.

Flipping through some of the alumni papers and pictures Kevin sighed and shook his head as he read one of the bios. "Did you read this one, Nicky?"

"Not yet, who is it?"

"Steve Johnson. I can't believe that he is married and has a kid. My God! I thought for sure he was gay. He was in every freaking play and every choir concert. Not that I am stereotyping him, but even Nic thought it. Right, Nicky? All those damn photos in the yearbook."

Nic remember it well. It became the running joke during yearbook to try to find a photo from any concert or play without Steve front and center.

"Did you really think he was gay, Nic?" Carmen asked.

"Yes I did." Nic laughed in agreement.

"But you remember who didn't think that and was totally smitten with him don't you?"

A chill ran down Nic's spine, he did indeed remember who had a crush on their former friend; Jenny. He knew it would happen sooner or later and had actually expected it sooner, and here it was; the first mention of Jenny.

"Of course . . ." Kevin continued. "That was before she fell madly in love with Bob; the brain dead idiot."

"Kevin!" Carmen swatted Kevin's hand and then sheepishly met Nic's eyes. "Look, I know she isn't the nicest person in the word, especially to you Nic; she has been my friend for a very long time. She does have her good side; she just doesn't show it often to others."

"Good side? Which one of her many sides is that?"

"Kevin! Stop!" Carmen said seriously but at the same time holding back her own laughter. "Kevin, she can't help her size. As for Bob, yes, I admit he isn't the brightest person in the world, but he does adore her."

"Well of course he does. He's worried that she'd beat the shit out of him."

Nic enjoyed watching the dialog between Kevin and Carmen; it was obvious that Kevin was doing everything in his power to put her down while Carmen was attempting to stay as neutral as possible. Kevin was saying all the things Nic had always wanted to say. Was he saying them for Nic's sake or did he truly feel the same?

"Kevin, please stop. Jenny has been very good to us." She turned her attention to Nic and took his hand in hers. "I know that she has been very cruel to you in the past and that something happened between you at the wedding. And for that I am very angry with her, but at the same time I can't . . ."

"Carmen, please don't concern yourself." Nic broke in. "Jenny and I will never be close. I know that you are; that doesn't change my feelings for you and Kevin."

Kevin downed the last of his wine. "Okay. We are getting far too serious here. Let's get out of here and have some fun!"

Nic glanced at his watch, he had an early class in the morning and it was already later than he normally would be out. However, he didn't want the evening to end. Carmen suggested they go dancing; she and Kevin hadn't been in months. Nic knew of only a few clubs in town so they ended up at the one that catered to a joint gay and straight audience. He and Christian would hang out here with friends or dates after classes because they both thought it played the best music and was completely smoke free.

Carmen immediately slipped her arm through Nic's and pulled him to the dance floor; it was exactly like the old days; the two of them dancing at the schools while their friends sat out. Kevin joined them for a short time but bored easily and needed a drink. Carmen watched her husband head to the bar and once she was satisfied that he would be fine she wrapped her arms around Nic and they danced even more enthusiastically.

"Finally! Some one who can keep up with me!"

"I'm a little out of practice so don't hold it against me if I bow out soon too."

"We'll see about that, Nicky!"

The adrenaline and energy of the music pulsed through them and they lost themselves in the seemingly endless dance. Nic lost track of time after a while but soon the weight of the night was taking its toll and he grew tired. He looked into Carmen's eyes and saw the same reflection of tiredness. This time he put his arm into hers and they pushed their way through the crowd.

"Oh Nicky, that was wonderful. I haven't danced like that in years."

"It was amazing. Christian and I come here occasionally with friends but I never dance like this. I've forgotten how much fun it is."

They returned to the bar and looked for Kevin.

"See your husband anywhere?"

"No. I was too busy dancing with my old dance partner." She laughed. "I bet he's gone to bathroom, he had more to drink than normal tonight. Either that or he's talking some poor guy's ear off about football."

"Probably."

"I am so glad to have you back in my life Nicky. I've missed you."

Kevin

Kevin checked his reflection in the mirror; he examined his nose carefully. He sniffed a few times and checked his nose a third time. He wanted to make sure Carmen and Nic wouldn't notice anything.

He leaned back from the mirror and noticed the man still waiting.

"It was good stuff, right? I told you it was the best." The man said.

"Excellent!" Kevin replied.

The man came closer till his face was just inches from Kevin's. He placed his hand on Kevin's crotch.

"This was good too."

"Thanks." Kevin kissed the man and then pulled away. "You weren't bad either. Maybe we'll meet again sometime."

"I'd like that. I guess you'd better get back before the wife misses you."

Kevin tapped his nose.

"Thanks again."

David

The last time he hiked these trails they had been covered in the last snow of the season. It had been cold and wet but Ben and Sarah were determined that if going for a walk was what he needed then they would put up with the discomfort. The three of them froze their asses off, but it was worth it.

Today, however, the trails were bursting with color. The trees shone bright green and the wildflowers were blooming in soft yellows, blues and purples. David felt as if nature was reaffirming the love and beauty of life. Everything had been going so perfectly lately; his father was moving out of state, Christian and Nic were coming home every weekend now, and of course he and Ben were still very much in love.

"How much farther to the lake?"

He'd been so enthralled in the beauty around him David had forgotten that Nic was even with him.

"Not much."

In the past month he and Ben had rapidly discovered a true friend in Nic. He'd offered the guys an ear as well as unconditional support. He answered their questions (even the ones they thought were stupid and had been embarrassed to ask), shared experiences from his own coming out, and suggested books, movies and music. Though they had access to so much information via the Internet, they liked having an actual person telling them some of the stuff. Ben worried at first that Nic would feel bothered by their constant barrage of questions; however Nic assured them that he wasn't. He told them he liked all the attention; he felt like a big gay brother giving advice to his little gay brothers.

"Next Thursday's the big night; are you getting nervous?"

"Yeah. I can't believe that Ben and I are going to our first dance together. Of course, we're not ready to make it public so we'll be keeping much of our affection hidden, but at least Sarah and Christian will know. For me, just the fact that Ben will be by my side is more than enough."

"So Ben's warming up to the idea of the dance? I know he said he didn't want to go before."

"He's been slowly growing more excited. He's still struggling with the idea that we are going together but that we won't be letting anyone else know."

"I can understand his feelings." Nic pushed some branches out of his way. "I went to my prom pining for someone I couldn't touch. Of course your situation is different, but I get the idea."

David stopped walking. "Your friend Kevin, right?"

Nic nodded his head in agreement. He leaned against the nearest tree, pulled his water bottle out and took a drink.

"Like I said, my situation was different, but still when I think about that night I think of it as a right of passage; something I had to go through. I wasn't happy at first, but once I got with my other friends I realized that I would have been more upset if I hadn't gone."

"Did you see Kevin there?"

"Absolutely." Nic smiled as he remembered the event. "I can still see him and Carmen dancing lovingly across the floor; oblivious to everyone around them. They looked so beautiful together. At the time I wished it was me in his arms."

Nic stopped for a moment and then met David's eyes. "You will actually be with Ben. So you guys aren't going to be shouting it from the roof tops that you're a couple, but you can still dance with him during the fast dances. Besides, I think I know you both enough now to know that you will find ways to show each other your love."

"Yeah, we will." David agreed, it was true they were doing it every day in school.

Nic tossed David his water bottle. David gulped down some and tossed it back. Nick pushed off the tree and they continued their trek through the woods.

"Any word from Ben's parents about your and Ben's plans to go to the cabin?"

"Oh yeah, I almost forgot." David said eagerly. "They finally said yes. I can hardly believe it."

"That is great. I am very envious. I have never had a getaway with someone before."

"Seriously?"

Nic playfully slugged his arm. David didn't mean it the way it sounded. He just assumed that Nic had probably had a relationship or two where they at least went away together for a weekend or something.

"Yes. What have you heard from Sarah? Has she been spreading rumors about me?"

"No, I swear."

Nic laughed. "Alas, sadly none of my boyfriends and I ever had the chance to go away together."

David was quite for a moment. He wanted to tell Nic about how nervous he was about their planned trip to the cabin. He and Ben had experimented with sex but they had always had to be careful as almost always there was the possibility of discovery from parents. This was going to be different though; Ben's parents were allowing them to go the cabin by themselves for a whole week. Sure they had plans to go hiking, shopping and dinner; but they'd be all by themselves with no possible interruptions, they'd be able to finally explore all the things they'd been wanting to.

"What is it?" Nic asked.

"I'm so anxious about the trip. It's a whole week away. We finally get to be, you know . . . alone."

"Oh, of course. But don't stress yourself out with anxiety. Enjoy your time now and when you both are together, it will make it all the more special."

"Thanks. Now come on, the lake is just around the next bend. Be prepared, it will take your breathe away."

Benjamin

George Washington High School had been holding its proms in the same party house since before anyone could remember; it was located in one of the nicer areas of town but it did have one major downside, its decor. The majority of the halls were still decorated in the bright yellows, orange, avocado green and brown colors so popular in the seventies. Luck was on their side as their prom was being held in the one room that had been redecorated. Instead of the garish colors they had all been expecting they found themselves in a room decorated in creams, tans and white. The red and gold streamers, balloons, flowers, and tablecloths were not trying to hide the awful colors but were actually enhancing the room.

Sarah gasped audibly. Christian stood wide eyed in disbelief. David lent into Ben's shoulder and whispered. "Aren't you glad you came? This place is fantastic."

Ben nodded; he was glad that he had come. He had remembered past proms, the class' chosen colors clashed so badly with the decor that aside from table cloths, they had almost no decorations at all. He liked to think that perhaps this was a sign that this night would be perfect.

"This is sharp." Christian said softly.

Ben watched as everyone nodded an agreement. His eyes rested on

David as the candle light twinkled in his green eyes. Ben felt an enormous happiness. Though he wouldn't act on his desires to pull David into his arms and kiss him, he would make the most of this night.

"Hey guys!"

Ben and David turned towards the sound of James' voice; he and Stephanie were walking towards them. Stephanie and Sarah hugged as the guys shook hands. Chuck and his girlfriend Holly joined them as the greetings were taking place.

"I've got us the best table in the place, close to the food and the dance floor, but farthest from the teachers and chaperons." Stephanie announced as she pointed to a table.

"Dudes! Where are the dates?" Chuck nudged David and Ben.

"We're going solo tonight. That way we have our pick of the best." David smirked as he pretended to check out the girls passing by while actually placing an arm around Ben's shoulders and giving a quick squeeze.

"Good thinking. Of course, for a couple of days now I was expecting to arrive and find you know who on your arm Ben. Even after Sarah's little stunt in homeroom I heard she was still telling people you were taking her."

"Yeah." Ben said bitterly.

James slugged Chuck's shoulder; it wasn't a playful one either.

"What? Chuck yelled as he rubbed his shoulder.

"Dumb ass; haven't you learned anything? You do not mention the psycho." James rolled his eyes.

Even though Ben knew Chuck was joking, Karen was a subject he would have preferred not hearing about tonight. It had been hard enough walking through school the past couple of days as people were stopping him and asking about the rumor. Most people didn't believe it, but they still wanted his take on the situation. During band yesterday o fellow saxophonist made a joke about it and when James saw the look of anger on Ben's face he cut in and told the classmate to drop the subject. Later when he and James were talking he asked him why he cut in. James told him he'd only seen a more evil look once before in his life and it was when his dad learned he'd dented the car; he didn't want their fellow band mate to suffer as much as he had.

"Let's take our seats. Come on." Sarah added quickly.

"Yes, let's sit down." Stephanie took James' arm and led him to the table.

Maneuvering to their table, David placed an innocent hand on Ben's back, pretending to direct him, however Ben knew that it meant more than that. Ben chose a seat nearest the wall where it would be more difficult for people to see him. He and David sat and instantly their hands were under the table cloth and intertwined. With David's hand tightly grasped in his, he felt so happy to be with the one he loved and surrounded by his closest friends. It was going to be a great night; he knew it.

Nicholas

Nic pushed his way through the smoky crowd; he coughed a few times and knew the stale smell of cigarette smoke and sweat were already permeating his clothes and hair. He longed for the smokeless bar back on campus but he had promised Donna they could go where ever she wanted tonight. He should have known that she would suggest The Vulture; it was the first gay bar they had ever gone to when they first came out. He could still remember the night they drove around searching for the dive. He'd been so surprised that the bouncer didn't even ask for their ID and wished them a good time. They spent more time in the place than either wanted to admit during those first few months; it was now regaled as a part of their history. When Donna chose it he almost didn't believe it was still in existence.

He checked his watch again, it was 9:45 and they had agreed to meet at 9:30; Donna was running late, as usual. He checked the bar for her as he ordered a beer. He took the beer and pushed his way towards the dance floor. He had always loved to watch the crowd dancing before and easily found his old favorite spot to gawk. Songs sped by before he felt the familiar tap on his shoulder. Donna kissed his cheek and whispered an apology for her lateness.

They exchanged a quick smile and left the dance floor and inched their way to the benches and booths at the back. They found an empty bench and sat; at least here they could talk without having to scream.

Donna lighted a cigarette. "Did you get the kids off okay?"

"Yeah! They looked great too. Ben and David are wearing matching tuxedos but David's tie and cumber bun is red while Ben's is white. Their boutonnieres are the reverse colors too. They looked so adorable and cute."

"I'll bet they did. They get to do something we never got to do. They're going to the prom with the person they truly want to be with."

Nic agreed; though he thought they also had it even better than he and Donna did in that they were surrounded by friends who truly cared for them and didn't care that they were a couple. Nic was glad to be included in that group.

"Our prom wasn't that awful; went together."

"True; however I wanted to go with Kimberly Barron and you were pining after Kevin. We were happy to be together but we were also miserable. Or have you blocked those memories?"

"No, I remember them." He placed an arm around Donna's shoulders and they leaned into each other and he placed his head on her shoulder. "Though I would never have admitted this then, I am very glad that I went with someone I love too."

Donna looked down at him and eyed him with suspicion. They shared a quickly laugh and returned to their people watching. They had spent so many nights in the past doing exactly what they were doing now. Nic was enjoying the old routine but he was even happier to be spending time with Donna; despite the smoke. He politely declined the offers of attractive men asking him to dance. He was quick to point out that he was at the bar with his friend.

"You can dance with someone if you are interested."

"I know, but most of these people want more than a dance. One night stands are not my thing. Besides I am here with you and I don't want to be out too late."

"Oh that's right; you've got big plans tomorrow. I hoped you were mine all night?"

"Sorry sweetie. I told you I promised Christian I would stay at the hotel with them tonight. You could join us. I'm sure the others wouldn't mind, especially Ben and David; they already think the world of you."

"Thanks, but no. I'll let you have your fun tonight. Next time though, I get you for at least 24 hours. Got it?"

"Deal!"

David

David and Sarah were dancing to one of their favorite songs, "Right Here Waiting" by Richard Marx; it was old and cheesy but it had been played at every dance they had ever attended and became a tradition for them to dance to it. Sarah had been dancing with Christian but the moment the song came on she abandoned Christian and pulled David to the dance floor without a word.

"Only you would pull me away in the middle of a conversation to dance."

Sarah smiled. "It's our song. You know that you and I will be dancing to this song at my wedding and every formal gathering we will ever have don't you? Even yours and Ben's wedding."

"I'll be sure to tell our DJ that this song is on our do not play list." He teased. "So a wedding, huh? I thought you were against weddings; you keep saying you and Christian were going to Vegas to elope and be married by Elvis."

"I know how much you and Ben can't wait to see me wed in the tackiest place imaginable, I've recently been thinking about how wonderful it would be to get married in my parent's hotel. We have people doing it all the time and they always look so elegant and glamorous."

David stopped dancing. "Who are you? What have you done with Sarah?"

"Stop it, David!" I do like to be glamorous sometimes; like tonight for example." She spun in his arms letting the dark plum dress shimmer as it caught the lights of the dance floor. Her blond curls dangled and danced as she spun again. David had to admit she did look very elegant and sophisticated tonight. If he had to use one word it would be breathtaking.

"There is no denying that you look amazing. So what changed your mind about the wedding?"

She shook her head no and held her lips tight.

"What?"

"I'm not going to tell you. You'll laugh at me."

"Come on, it's me your talking to. I know more about you than I could possibly imagine. What more could you say to make me laugh?"

"It's embarrassing. Even I can't believe something so silly made me think so strongly about it that it actually changed my mind."

Their song ended and was replaced with one they both hated; Whitney Houston's horrid rendition of "I Will Always Love

You". They both stopped dancing the moment it began and cringed. They could see all their friends and classmates crowding the floor; they hurried in the opposite direction towards the refreshment counter. They each took a bottle of water and Sarah started to drink. David knew she was trying to avoid continuing their conversation; he wasn't going to let her get away so easily.

"Come on, the guys are waiting." He took her hand and led her back towards the table. "So what was it that was so silly?"

"No! David, I am not telling you."

"You have to tell me. You can't expect me not to ask, especially after your brought it up. Was it Christian? Your parents? Did Ben say something?"

"No, it was Nic."

"Nic? Oh what did Nic say? Did he ask you if you wanted . . .?"

"No." She broke in. "Nic and I were watching some clips of an old TV show on YouTube."

"TV? Okay . . . so let me guess . . . could it be . . ."

"You'll never guess the show in a million years. It hasn't been on the air since the 80's and as far as I know it is not being rerun anywhere at the moment. That is as much as I am willing to share."

"Sarah, please? You can't leave me hanging like this. Please? Please?" David pleaded.

"Oh fine. It was *Dynasty*. Nic was watching all these clips a couple weeks ago and he got me hooked watching with him. One of the clips was this wedding and it looked so beautiful. Yes, of course the styles were hideous with those enormous shoulder pads but the look and feel of it was so elegant. It got me thinking that perhaps I was . . ."

Sarah stopped mid sentence; David stumbled a moment, it wasn't like Sarah to stop unless someone interrupted her. He looked at her and noticed that she was staring straight ahead towards their table. David turned his attention to the table and saw why she stopped talking; Karen was talking to Ben. He could see that Ben was trying to ignore her but she didn't seem to want to leave.

"Damn it!"

He tightened his grip on Sarah's hand and pulled her towards the table with him. It had taken him and Sarah days to convince Ben that prom would not be a waste of time and that despite the rumor mill; they would have a wonderful evening. Ben shared that he didn't know if he could manage another dance where he would have to pretend to be someone he wasn't. They had convinced him that Karen wouldn't dare show her face after Sarah's act in homeroom; he never expected her to really show up.

Karen saw David and Sarah approach the table and David could see the panic in her eyes. He could only guess that she had hoped to have Ben on the floor with her before they returned.

"Please Ben, just one dance? I came here tonight, like, to just dance with you."

"No. Leave me alone." Ben said angrily.

David knew from the tone of Ben's voice that he was close to his breaking point. Damn it, why did Karen have to show up tonight."

"Ben, please just one dance with me?"

"Look miss!" Christian said sternly. "Ben said no. I think it would be best if you left him alone. Okay?"

"Ben? Ben, please don't hurt my feelings tonight. One dance - that is all I am asking."

"Karen! He doesn't want to dance with you. Please go!" David pleaded.

"Benji! Don't do this to me!" Karen was practically screaming and people at nearby tables were beginning to take notice of the exchange. "Please? Please Benji?"

Ben rose so quickly from his chair that it rocked back and fell to floor with a bang. Karen gasped and Sarah and Stephanie flinched.

Ben's brow tightened, his lips were drawn tight and his hands balled at his said.

"I said NO!" He didn't look at Karen or his friends; he started walking towards the nearest exit.

Karen was about to go after him, but James reached out and grabbed her arm.

"Leave him alone! God, get it into your fucking head that he doesn't want you dumb-shit!"

"Benji! Benji!" Karen screamed.

Ben didn't stop and David knew that he was trying to get out of the room as quickly as possible. He knew it was killing him to know everyone was watching the spectacle now. He would wait until Ben left the hall and then hurry after him.

"I love you Benji! I LOVE YOU!"

Ben stopped with a jerk. Slowly he spun on his heels and faced Karen. David could see the anger on his flushed faced. He was about to blow.

"Leave . . . me . . ." Ben was forcing each word out with controlled anger. "The FUCK ALONE!"

Ben's lips quivered and his shoulders shook. His eyes only moved from Karen to David. His anger deflated and he hurried the room.

Karen pushed James way from her and ran out the room. David and Sarah shared worried glances. He knew what he had to do. "I'll bring him back."

Nicholas

A hand waved in front of his face and Nic shifted uncomfortably. It took him a moment to realize that it was Donna's. They hadn't talked for a bit and he had let himself become enthralled in the music and the crowd that he hadn't realized that she had been talking.

"You still with us?"

He'd been watching two people dance and he couldn't help but think he recognized the one. He shook his head.

"Sorry about that . . . it's just . . ."

Donna looked towards the crowd trying to figure out what was keeping his attention.

"Nic? What in the world are you staring at? If you want to dance don't let me hold you back."

"No . . . no . . . no."

"What is it?"

He lifted his arm and pointed into the crowd. "Over there, dancing with the bleach blond with the spiked hair."

"There has to be at least ten boys matching that description. I need something more than that."

Nic stood and pulled Donna up and turned her towards the crowd.

He stood behind her and pointed over her shoulder.

"There; dancing with the blond in the green shirt. See the guy in the red shirt."

"What? I don't . . . oh, oh my God! Is that . . ."

"Kevin? Yes, it is; unless he has an identical twin we don't know about."

"What's he doing here and where is . . ."

"His wife?" Nic finished her thought. What should he do? Should he approach Kevin? It didn't make any sense; Kevin had never been a huge fan of dancing, but looking at him now Nic would have never guessed that. He also would not have thought he was straight; the grinding of waists and the way he and the blond were hanging on each seemed to contradict that.

"Holy shit! Look at the two of them. What the hell is he doing?"

"I don't know. Why is he here? Hey?"

Nic stopped as he noticed the blond whisper into Kevin's ear. A smile crossed Kevin's face and the two wrapped arms around each others shoulders and left the dance floor. They were heading towards the restrooms.

Without thinking, Nic left Donna's side and started to follow them.

"Nic, wait!" Donna held onto his arm. "Do you think you should really go after him? Who knows what you are going to see. Do you want to put yourself through that?"

"I have to know Donna. I need to know why he is here."

He gave her a look of determination. After all he had been through with Kevin this was something he couldn't let pass.

"All right. I'll be here waiting. Be careful Nic."

He couldn't explain it any clearer. He had to find out what Kevin was doing here, but it wasn't for the reason he assumed Donna thought. It wasn't because he was hoping Kevin might be gay and a future could somehow develop for them. It was Carmen. In the months since the wedding, he and Carmen had gotten close again and he had re-discovered a dear friend and he didn't want her hurt.

Karen

Where is he? Where did he go? She knew he came outside so he had to be in the parking lot, right? Maybe he went to his car? What car was it again? She couldn't remember what car he'd arrived in. She'd been sitting in her car waiting for him to arrive so she could see if he came with a date or not. Oh why couldn't she remember what car was his.

She knew that Benji had only done and said the things he did because Sarah and David had approached the table. If they hadn't come back when they did Benji would have gladly gotten up and danced with her. How could he not, especially after she'd bought such a wonderful dress for him? She only had to find him and get him alone; he'd tell her the truth. He wouldn't want to leave this situation with her the way he had. It was David and Sarah's fault that he reacted the way he did. Why couldn't they understand that she and Benji loved one another and that they were bringing them unhappiness? Why did they have to be so mean and force their dislike of her on him? She wouldn't give up though; she knew she and Benji belonged together. She would show Sarah and David what true love was and prove to them how happy she could make Benji. She scanned the lot again; he had to be around here somewhere. She knew he wouldn't leave without apologizing to her.

Wait a minute there was David, why was he coming out now? Damn it! He was going to ruin everything. He couldn't find Benji before she did. No. She had to find him first. Darn. Maybe he would go back inside if he didn't see her. She hid behind a car and watched him search.

She could see that David was heading towards the back of the hall; she continued to hide from view behind cars and inched her way to towards the back. As she got closer she saw that Benji was indeed behind the hall; he was pacing angrily. Damn, David found him first! No. No. No.

David neared and the two appeared to say something to each other before they hugged. Benji looked like he was crying. She wanted to run forward and shove David away so she could be the one to provide him with comfort. She knew that he was crying because he was upset that he hurt her.. She hoped that David would be the bigger man and tell him to go and find her and tell her he was sorry. David knew that Benji loved her and they belonged together.

She was about to rise from her place and was about to join them when she noticed that David said something to Benji and they were laughing. Was he telling Benji to go to her? Benji was smiling; it had to be that, right? Wait . . . what was David doing? David was placing his hands on Benji's cheeks and he . . no . . . it couldn't be that . . . he was kissing Benji. No! Why wasn't Benji pushing him away? No, he was pulling David closer and kissing him back.

This was not happening. Benji was being forced to do it. This was David's fault. He was forcing his disgusting ways on Benji and she would not stand for it. She would not give Benji up without a fight. If David thought he could force himself on Benji and not be punished he would regret it. Benji loved her; not him. He was going to pay for this and pay dearly.

Nicholas

Nic entered the bathroom; he had expected Kevin and the blond to be in a stall not out in the place sight. They were too involved with each other to notice him. Kevin was leaning against a wall as the blond had his back to Nic; they were snorting something. Nic could only guess what they were doing; the drugs didn't bother him as much as the savage way the two began to kiss afterward. Kevin was panting heavily and began to push the blond to his knees where he began to unzip Kevin's pants.

"Huh-huh!" Nic cleared his throat before the blond could begin.

Kevin's eyes slowly opened; he looked around innocently until he noticed Nic and his eyes widened with surprise and shock. He pushed the other man away and fumbled with his zipper.

"What the fuck are you doing?" The blond said. He noticed Nic standing inside the door. "Who's this, the boyfriend?" He shrugged and returned his hands to Kevin's pants. "Get lost and find yourself someone to play with."

"Shut up!" Kevin swatted the blonde's hands away. "Get out!"

The blond glanced between Nic and Kevin. "Screw this." He pushed his way past Nic.

Nic hadn't moved since he announced his presence. He stood

rigidly at the entrance with his hands hanging at his side. He tried not to look disgusted by what he'd seen, but he also didn't want Kevin to think that he approved of what he'd seen.

Kevin shifted uncomfortably and attempted to laugh but when Nic didn't respond he finished adjusting his pants nervously. He looked around the room several times and wrung his hands. Nic could guess that he was trying to find a way to get out of this situation.

"Nicky, look I know how this looks. But believe me its not that bad."

Nic resisted the urge to throttle his friend and stood his ground. He knew that his silence was worst for Kevin than anything he could actually say at the moment.

"Come on Nicky . . . I mean, you can't tell me that you haven't acted on desires before. All we have to do is look at what happened between us in high school. Seriously, look at how bad you wanted it to . . ."

Nic didn't even realize he was moving until he was shoving Kevin against the wall. In his drugged up and nervous state Kevin was taken completely off guard.

"Don't you dare compare what happened between us to what you were just doing?" Nic screamed in Kevin's face. "We were in high school! We didn't know any better!"

Kevin rubbed his shoulder and tried to push away from the wall but Nic was stronger and didn't budge. Kevin tried again more aggressively but again Nic easily kept him pinned to the wall.

"Fuck you Nic! Don't act all superior to me. You had no fucking problem screwing around then. I don't owe you any explanation. Fuck off!"

"That's right; you don't owe me anything!" Nic pulled away allowing Kevin to finally leave the wall. "You don't owe me anything, but there is someone you do owe an explanation to!"

"What?"

"Carmen - you dumb shit. Tell me, does she know about your little desires?"

Kevin didn't answer at first. He meet Nic's stare and for the first time Nic could actually see fear in them.

"Nicky, look . . . I know that you don't understand but sometimes I need more . . . more than she can give me."

"That explains the sex, but what about the stuff you snorted up your nose?"

Nic watched Kevin's fear grow. This was the person he had once held in such high regard and had emulated so much. Even after everything that happened between them he still couldn't hate Kevin even when he said he did. These past couple of months Nic had been so happy to have his friend back, but now he saw Kevin clearly. It had all been an elaborate ruse. The selfish, egotistical asshole had finally shown his true colors. Nic wondered if anyone had ever been able to see the real Kevin.

"Nicky, please don't look at me like that. I know that I fucked up here, but we can move past this. We can pretend it never happened."

"It won't work this time, Kevin."

"Nicky, it's been so good to have you back in my life again . . ." He moved slightly and let his hand fall and he grabbed Nic's crotch. "We can do it your way . . ."

Nic slapped his hand away.

"Come on Nicky! Let me show you how good it can be between us."

It took all Nic's strength not to punch Kevin in the face. Instead he shoved him back into the wall.

"Nicky, please? Don't do this. I've missed you. I want you . . ."

"Stop it! My God, do you really think I am that ignorant? All my life Kevin there has been this small part of me that has always cared and loved you. Even with all the bullshit you gave me that little something kept beating. I was so happy when I got that invitation; I thought, finally we can put the past behind us. You said everything I wanted to hear. I wonder if you ever truly meant any of it. Were you ever really my friend?"

"Of course. I meant all of it. I swear."

"I don't believe you. This is more than I can or want to take. That little part of me that has always cared for you has finally died; it is gone. I can't stand to look at you."

"Don't say that, Nicky. Please?" Kevin pleaded with tears flowing down his cheeks. "Please Nic, I need you."

Nic slowly backed away from Kevin until his back was touching the exit. He gripped the handle and opened the door, his eyes never leaving Kevin's.

"I feel sorry for you. No, wait; I take that back. I feel sorry for Carmen. I hope she never learns what a fucking jerk you truly are."

Nic left the room and ignored the cries of help and forgiveness he could hear Kevin screaming. He returned to Donna who was waiting eagerly where he left her. He held out his hand and she took it. He led her out of the bar. Once outside he stopped and took a deep breathe as the realization of what happened finally hit him.

"What happened, Nic?"

"Let's just say that for the first time I finally discovered who the real Kevin is?"

Donna wrapped Nic in her arms.

"I'm sorry."

"Me too."

Benjamin

Friday 7:00 am

Despite the unexpected arrival of the Psycho at prom and my inevitable outburst, last night turned out to actually be a great night. David was my knight in shining armor coming to my rescue. When he found me out behind the hall, I was so angry and upset. I didn't think I could go back inside and face my friends or the crowds. David held me and told me that I had nothing to be concerned about - I wasn't the crazy one that caused a scene. I wanted us to leave right there and then. I told him that I wanted him to take me home and hold me in his arms. He said he would do that, but only after I went back and showed everyone that I wasn't going to let the bitch ruin my night. We both laughed and after a few more words of encouragement I agreed. It also took some kisses from David to make me completely agree. Okay, so yeah, I was still nervous but when David told me that he would be at my side for the rest of the night and beyond I knew he meant it.

David led me back inside with his arm around my shoulder and true to his word, he never left my side. Amazingly, lots of people came up and congratulated me; they said my outburst was awesome; some even told me that I had made their prom even more memorable. David was right there telling me there were right. I know this sounds crazy but I truly did have a wonderful time the rest of the night.

We got back to the hotel around 12:30 am; Nic was waiting for us in the suite Sarah's parents had reserved for us. We drank non-alcoholic champagne and filled him in on the events of the evening. Nic shared the events of his night as well. David and I were shocked to hear about what happened with his friend Kevin, but Nic said he felt relieved to have found out now and not years later. We all laughed about how ironic it seemed that both of us had crazy nights.

Sarah and Christian "retired" to their portion of the suite around 1:00 am but neither David nor I were tired yet so we decided to hang around the living room and were happy that Nic joined us. It was fantastic; David and I talked for the first time about what we were going to do after graduation next week. David doesn't want me to lose my scholarship so he wants to move with me to California and will take his year off hanging out with me instead of traveling. I know that it is a topic we should have been talking about earlier but I think both of us were scared to hear what the other might say. I know that David has dreamed about being able to travel ever since his grandparents left him money in their wills. I had actually been investigating if it was possible to delay my scholarship a quarter so we could do some traveling, but David said he didn't want me to do that. He wanted me to go as planned and that we were too important for him to think about traveling. He'd rather be with me than away from me. It was so beautiful to hear him say it, thought I am sure Nic must have thought us incredible sappy as we fawned over each other. We were dominating the conversation and I was worried about that since we were going away for the weekend and wouldn't see Nic for a bit, but he said he didn't mind. He said he liked living vicariously through us.

When we finally went to bed I felt immediately asleep in David's arms, but by 6:30 I was wide awake. I packed up the remainder of our clothes and got everything else ready for the trip. I managed to slip out of the room and ran down to my room and retrieved David's surprise. I can't wait for him to see it. It's not the same type of journal as this but more a testament to our friendship and love. I filled it with some stories I wrote, some poetry (sadly, yes some of them are my disastrous attempts), photos, and some clippings. I'd been contemplating what type of gift to give him and while so many ideas ran through my head from rings to dinner, but then I realized I wanted something more personal. I know he is going to love it. I am going to give it to him tonight after we arrive at the cabin. We're going to breakfast and then our annual after prom trip to putt-putt and then we're off. It is going to be a great day. I feel as if David and I are finally starting our real lives together today. Good things are coming.

Till later . . .

B-

Nicholas

Carmen had phoned the hotel earlier this morning telling the staff that it was an emergency that she speak with Nic. They had hesitated waking him, but the moment he heard who was on the line, he was glad they had. She wouldn't say much on the phone except that she had to see him and was on her way to the hotel. He asked her what had happened, but she wouldn't say and she hadn't said anything about Kevin, so he didn't ask. He told her he would be waiting in the lobby.

He dressed and was heading down the stairs and was surprised to see Carmen already waiting for him. Had she called from the parking lot? She didn't notice him at first so he took a moment to look her over. Her hair was a mess, she was dressed in sweats; her face was red and rough looking.

She noticed him and waved, nervously. He hurried down and she hugged him. He could see that she had been crying and the moment her head rested on his shoulder she softly sobbed. He patted her back and she pulled away and attempted to smile. He led her to a secluded sitting area.

Carmen sat and took a long deep breath; she held it for a moment and then let it out slowly. She wiped her eyes and nose.

"I . . . I know everything."

Her left hand took his and held it while her right hand dug in her pocket and produced a small vial filled with some white powder. Nic didn't recognize it but could guess what it held and whose vial it was.

"I know everything."

What did Carmen mean by everything? Was producing the vial a way to tell Nic that she learned Kevin was doing drugs? She couldn't possibly mean that she also knew about Kevin's infidelity too, right? He wanted to ask but at the same time he knew he had to be patient and let her tell him what she knew; it wasn't his place to tell her more than she might not know.

"What is it?"

Carmen's hand left his and gently cupped his chin.

"You don't have to protect him, Nicky. Kevin . . . Kevin told me everything last night . . . this morning. He told me how you confronted him in the bathroom of some bar."

Nic wanted to look away as he felt guilty. He didn't know why, but with Carmen in front of him he felt as if he should have been a better friend and phoned her last night.

"He did? Wow . . . I mean, Carmen, I wasn't sure it was . . ."

"I know that Nicky. Though I don't think you heard me; I know everything." She removed her hand from his chin and grasped both of his hands in hers. "Last night Kevin came home and sat me down and said he had to share something with me. He started with your relationship in high school. He finally admitted that he had some kind of feelings for you and knew that you felt the same way so he acted on them and you reciprocated. He said at the time he thought it was just two boys experimenting but then realized that you weren't experimenting so he freaked and pushed you out of his life. He said he didn't tell me the truth because he didn't think I could handle it."

Nic was dumbfounded. He couldn't believe that Kevin admitted it.

"He didn't stop there though." Carmen said. "He said that he was so mad at himself for liking what happened that he started doing drugs. He recited this whole list of things that he's tried over the years; weed, coke, meth, you name it. It was horrifying. But before I could even say anything he went on and started telling me about one night stands with women and men. He then had the audacity to say that despite all of that, he still loved me and wanted to be with me so that is why he wanted to get married."

"What?"

Carmen nodded and attempted another smile but instead dropped her head into her hands and cried. Nic left his seat across from her, joining her on the couch; he placed an arm around her shoulder.

"I'm sorry, Carmen. Truly I am."

"Nicky . . ." She wiped her tears. "There's still more."

He didn't believe it was possible but he continued to be shocked by Carmen's revelations. Kevin had told her that he first started doing drugs with Jenny and Bob. They had offered him something at a party and thought why not. Before he knew it, they were continually sneaking off when Carmen was at school or work getting stoned, high or tripping on something. Kevin even admitted to sleeping with Jenny on numerous occasions.

"Oh Nic, how could I have been so blind not to see any of this? Am I really that stupid?"

"No! Carmen, he had everyone fooled. It was a game to him and he played it perfectly."

Carmen nodded and genuine smile came to her face.

"Nicky, I am so sorry for what he did to you. I wish I had been stronger and knew . . ."

"Carmen, I'm the one who should be apologizing. I knew you and Kevin were dating but I still let it go on."

"Nicky that was high school! My God everyone experiments then. You have nothing to be ashamed or sorry for. Kevin should have been man enough to admit it and not treat his best friend like he did."

The two hugged again as they both shared tears of forgiveness.

"What are you going to do?"

"I don't know. I left the house and told him I wanted him gone by the time I get back. I . . . I don't know when I'm going back though or if I want to."

"I understand. I'm sure there is a room here at the hotel if you need it."

"I just might take you up on that. Thank you Nicky, for being here for me."

"My feelings for you haven't changed. If you need anything, please let me know."

"I . . . I need a friend."

"You've got it."

David

"Four!"

David glanced back at his friends as he swung his putter as if he was truly going to drive the little yellow ball through the park. He could see Ben snickering and Sarah rolling her eyes.

"I dare you! You'd never do it."

"I might surprise you, Sarah!"

"Not a chance on this one. So quit bluffing and just putt."

"Okay." David continued his swing and just before the putter made contact with the ball he stopped. He winked at Sarah and tapped the ball which went straight into the hole.

Sarah gasped. "I don't believe it! How in the world do you keep getting hole-in-ones? That is your fifth. I thought your kind didn't like golf?"

"Oh, like blonds can do any better?"

This opened the floodgates for an impromptu debate on athletic abilities between him and Sarah. She'd pose one argument and David would quickly counter; they were egging the other on to see how long they could keep it up. Ben and Christian stood in awe looking back and forth between them.

"Okay . . . okay . . . let's get back to the game" Christian said as he took Sarah's arm and led her to the next hole.

"This isn't over yet!" Sarah teased.

Ben placed a hand on David's lower back as they followed Christian and Sarah. "While I thoroughly enjoyed the display, you do realize that the longer this game takes, the longer it will be before we can hit the road. Then the longer it takes us to hit the road, the longer it will before we can . . . um, well you know."

"Maybe I'm enjoying dragging it out." David smirked. "The anticipation of what's to come might make it all the sweeter."

"This is it!" Sarah did her best Vanna White impression as she waved her arms in the air presenting them with the famed hole #17. It had been their favorite hole for as long as they had been coming here. It was shaped like a mountain and required the the putter to putt through a hole underneath and then to walk through a small passage in the mountain to reach the green. For Sarah, it held an even greater importance; it had been the place she and Christian had their first kiss. They liked to repeat it every time they played the hole too.

"As if you had to remind us. Go putt and we'll give you three minutes; no more!" Ben said.

Sarah and Christian both quickly putted then made their way to the passage. Ben pointed to his watch as Sarah looked back. Christian winked and pulled Sarah hungrily inside.

"What are we going to do with them?"

"As if we won't be doing the very same thing tonight when we get to the place we had our first kiss."

David knew that Ben was right; the cabin would be their special place where their memories would always draw them. He also couldn't wait to get there and kiss Ben.

Ben looked at his watch again, they had let more than three minutes pass. He placed his ball on the tee and putted.

"I'll go see if the coast is clear."

David put his ball down and started to swing.

"Leave him alone!"

David jumped; he hadn't expected anyone to be behind him as the course wasn't busy. He looked over his shoulder and was even more surprised to see Karen behind him. She held a putter in her hand and looked angry. Before he could ask her what she was doing here, he heard Ben ask her "what the hell she was doing".

Karen didn't respond to Ben, she kept her vision glued to David. It sent chills down his spine; he had never seen such rage before.

"Leave Ben alone!" Her voice was high and shaky.

"Get the hell out of here, Karen!" Ben yelled as he moved towards her.

"Ben, don't!" David held Ben from getting close to her. He could only imagine what would happen if Ben got mad enough to push her. Instead he looked at her and spoke. "Didn't you do enough with your little stunt last night? Get the hint and go away!"

"ME?" Karen's face flushed bright red; her whole body shook. She swung the putter out and struck David in the shin.

"Shit!" David yelled as he felt the putter make contact. He could feel the pressure throbbing through his entire leg. Had Ben not been right behind him he probably would have fallen down.

"What the fuck is wrong with you? I told you last night to leave me alone!"

The redness and rage vanished from Karen's face as she flashed the eeriest smile at Ben.

"Don't worry, Benji. I know, like, why you said those things last night." She turned her gaze back to David and the rage reappeared. "It is HIS fault!"

"What?"

"SHUT UP!" Karen swung the putter again and narrowly missed David's other leg. "You pervert! I saw what you did. I saw it and it made me sick."

Ben pulled David behind him as Karen now wielded the putter like a sword and was pointing it towards David's chest. David glanced around to see if anyone else was noticing what was happening; he saw Sarah and Christian standing several feet away but he didn't know if anyone else could see. He had hoped that perhaps the Putt-Putt staff were aware and calling the police or security. He had never seen such anger and confusion, even with his father; the rage in Karen's face and body was more terrifying.

"I saw what you did to my darling Benji last night. You, like, used him and turned him against me. We had something special and true between us and you are trying to ruin it."

"Karen, listen to me." Ben said slowly and calmly. "There was never anything between us. You have to understand . . ."

"Last night you forced yourself on him!" Karen continued as if Ben hadn't said a word. "You forced your disgusting kisses on him and made him kiss you back. You are vial!"

"Wait a fucking minute!" Ben's calmness was gone; he spoke with force and determination. "David did not force me to do anything that I didn't want to do. How dare you say anything to him or me about that? Get the fuck out of here!"

"Stop protecting him Benji." Karen said with her sugary sweetness. "He is evil and must be punished for corrupting you."

"No! I will never love you. I love David!"

"Benji, he is forcing you to say this." She appeared panic stricken now and she continued to swing the putter while going back and forth between smiles at Ben and looks of anger at David. "I know we . . . we belong . . . no . . . It's not possible . . . no . . ."

"I love David and I belong with him." Ben said softly.

Karen seemed to crack at Ben's response. She dropped the putter, fell to her knees and started to sob.

David inched closer to Ben, before he could even place a hand on his back, he could feel the shaking of his body. He looked around the park more thoroughly this time; Sarah and Christian still stood wide eyed and dumbfounded but were now joined by several other putters and staff.

"Please . . . please . . . tell me . . ." Karen spoke between sobs. "It can't . . . It's not true. Benji, please . . . please tell me . . ."

Ben's body stopped shaking and an aura of calmness seemed to come over him. David knew this was the moment Ben had been hoping for; Karen was finally listening to what he was going to tell her.

"It is true, Karen. I won't apologize for it either. I am not ashamed of my love." Ben's hand found David's and they were at each others side. "I love David and I am not ashamed or afraid to show it."

"No!" Karen whined.

Ben pulled David into his arms and kissed him with the sweetest passion they had ever shared before. David didn't care that they were out in public and that people were watching him; it was the sweetest and most pleasurable kiss he'd even had. It was gentle, relaxed and so full of love.

When their lips parted, David knew what pleasure and love truly was and he couldn't help but smile and was delighted to see it mirrored on Ben's face as well.

The kept their hands locked together as they walked away from Karen's slumping body. David could see the joy on Sarah's and Christian's faces. Sarah was bouncing up and down and cheering them on while Christian was clapping.

Time suddenly seemed to slow down as David noticed Christian's smile melt and his eyes widen; his mouth opened as if he was about to scream. David's brain registered that something was wrong; out of the corner of his eye he noticed something coming at him. He jerked and ducked just in time; he felt the brush of wind above his head. Before he could process the relief of being missed, he heard a deafening thud and he was pulled down to the ground. He was disoriented as he hit the ground. He could hear screams from all around him and he knew that people were running towards them but he couldn't focus quickly enough to know what was happening. After a moment or two he knew he was on the ground and Ben was still holding his hand but it wasn't until he heard Sarah screaming Ben's name that his disorientation disappeared. He pushed himself up from the ground to see Sarah and Christian at Ben's side.

"Ben? Ben? What happened? Ben?" David screamed.

"Someone help! Someone please help us!" Christian yelled.

"Oh God, Ben, please, please answer me."

"He isn't responding." Sarah cried.

Sarah

Silence had overtaken the private waiting room for such a long time now that Sarah felt as if she and David had been banished to a place where sound didn't exist. When they first arrived it had been filled with so much noise; chaotic talking and the unending questions. It seemed everyone needed to speak with her and David as they had been the ones to witness the event and the ones who arrived in the ambulance with Ben; first it had been the medical staff, then Mr. and Mrs. Tolliver, and then the police. David hadn't spoken a word since their ride in the ambulance, even as the nurses attempted to examine his leg he wouldn't say a word. The talking fell to Sarah; especially as she had seen the actual incident. She told the story so many times now that she didn't think she would ever forget it. Once the Tollivers were allowed to be with Ben and the police were satisfied with everything they heard, Sarah actually realized that Christian and Nic had joined them; she'd been so busy giving details to notice they were at her side.

Hours passed and while both Sarah and David had refused to leave she told Christian and Nic to go home and rest. Once they were alone, neither could bring themselves to say anything so they sat silently staring at a blank wall. Mr. Tolliver would come out every couple of hours and give them an update on Ben's condition; unconscious but in stable condition. As time passed the updates became surreal; it was as if they were hearing about someone other than Ben. The doctors were saying that Ben had TBI: Traumatic Brain Injury. His brain was swelling and they weren't sure how severe the damage was yet. TBI? What the hell is that? It didn't make any sense. How was it possible that Ben was suffering from something that sounded like something she'd see on *Grey's Anatomy* or *House*? It had been almost 12 hours since Ben had been brought in and yet the doctors still couldn't determine how sever the damage was? How was that possible?

She had wanted to scream just to break the silence that seemed to be choking them. She felt so helpless sitting here doing nothing. Though she was feeling helpless, she couldn't help but notice how utterly lost David appeared. He rose from his chair and walked to the glass doors that separated the waiting room from the depths of the emergency room. He placed his palm to the glass. He'd done this about a dozen times already. Sarah could only imagine that he was attempting to will all his strength to find Ben and heal him. David turned and Sarah held out her hand; he grasped it and returned to his seat. It was the first time that since they entered the waiting room that he didn't release it after sitting down. He squeezed gently and she could see that tears were falling rolling down his cheeks again.

She didn't want to but she found herself once again recalling the events that lead them to this spot. Ben had looked so happy and relieved as he kissed David. She had never been more proud of the two of them. The months of hiding were gone and both of them seemed to carry themselves with a new sense of pride. Ben's smile was so big and bright and contagious. She couldn't help but smile as well. When Christian started clapping she wanted to run and hug her friends and tell them how happy she was for them. She took one step and noticed Karen had risen from the ground. She opened her mouth to yell a warning but it all happened so fast. Before she could say anything she noticed David duck. She saw the putter narrowly miss David's head and continue its swing; then Ben's head whipped violently to the side. As the clank of the putter sounded she heard herself scream.

The next few minutes were a blur; she remembered running to Ben's side, but then nothing until she was in the ambulance. She didn't remember how she gotten there or when the paramedics arrived, she merely remembered staring at Ben's head as one of the EMT was taking vitals. It wasn't until after all the questioning and she was in Christian's arms that she learned she had demanded she and David be allowed in the ambulance. She also learned Karen had not escaped as other customers at the Putt-Putt ran to their aid and held her until the police arrived.

She shook the images from her head; she didn't want to think about it again. She couldn't go through it again. She wanted to think positively.

She laid her head on David's shoulder. She allowed her eyes to close and her body easily gave into sleep.

She jerked awake some time later as David gently shook her. She looked around and noticed that Mr. Tolliver was walking down the hall towards them. David took a quick intake of breath and stiffened. Mr. Tolliver was walking slowly and heavily. His eyes were teary and red.

"Sarah . . . David. . ."

Mr. Tolliver knelt and took their hands into his.

"The damage was . . . it was worse . . . he . . . Ben . . . Ben didn't make it."

PART THREE

David

In the days since the attack it seemed as if God was punishing them; storm clouds rolled in bringing heavy rain, thunder, lightening, and hail. It was if the heavens had opened up in protest to the injustice of Ben's passing. The sky had turned from sunny and bright to a dark gloomy gray. Today was going to be hard enough for him, but to have to deal with such weather just made it all the more difficult. He wanted to curl back into bed, wrap a blanket over his head and hide away from everything. He didn't want to do this.

His mother knocked on his door.

"David. Finish tying your tie. We have to leave in a little bit."

He nodded an agreement. He wasn't sure how long he'd been standing in front of the mirror. He looked at himself but didn't see his reflection but memories of good times. He could see Ben and him dancing on his first night back in his room after his father moved out, he saw them lying in bed talking about the future, and he saw Ben pinning the boutonniere on David's tux just a couple of nights ago. He looked away from the mirror before the bad memories returned.

David picked up his suit jacket and pulled it on. He sat on the edge of the bed wondering how he could possibly go through this. It had been hell yesterday even with Sarah, Christian, and Nic with him. When he stood at the entrance to the room where Ben was laid out he hadn't been able to move. Nic had to physically pull him into the room. The moment Mrs. Tolliver saw them she pulled them into her arms and hugged them tightly. She was crying and telling them how much Ben loved him and Sarah and how she couldn't have asked for better friends for her son.

He didn't know how she and Mr. Tolliver were able to move around the room greeting people. Mrs. Tolliver looked as if she had been crying for months while Mr. Tolliver looked as if he hadn't slept in days; yet they were able to move around the room. David could barely get out of bed let alone shower without being pushed. His whole body was numb and lifeless. The most important person in his life had been stolen away from him.

The worst part of the viewing was the casket itself; it was open. Though a small part of him still wanted to see Ben, a bigger part of him wanted it to be closed so he could pretend it wasn't him. He didn't have the option not to see it, Sarah took his hand in hers and before he knew it she had led him right to it. For a moment David didn't feel anything. Ben was just there with closed eyes; he looked as if he was sleeping. However the longer they stood there and despite the funeral parlors best effort; he could still the see the discoloration where the impact had happened. The sickeningly sweet mixture of flowers, makeup and embalming fluid was too much; David knew Ben was truly gone. His knees gave out and the tears he hadn't shed since the hospital when Mr. Tolliver told them what happened came pouring out. Nic and Christian were behind him and helped him to his feet and to a chair where he remained for the rest of the night; his eyes never leaving Ben's face. He couldn't go through that again; it was too much. He didn't want to see Ben like that.

His mother returned.

"David, are you ready to go?"

He didn't answer her. She sat next to him and placed a motherly hand on his.

"Darling, I know this is hard for you to understand right now, but this is something you need to do. I wish you didn't have to go through it and I know it is unfair, but Ben wouldn't want you to stop living. He'd want you to go on and be happy. You have to do this."

David shook his head.

"If you don't do this, you will regret it later. Believe me, you don't want that."

Regret it? Was she fucking nuts? Didn't she know he couldn't say goodbye to Ben? He had been the one thing in David's life that had taken away all the pain and the fears and replaced them with warmth, joy and love. How could he say goodbye to that? Life didn't seem important without Ben by his side. No, she wasn't nuts; he knew she was right; no matter how screwed up it was, he had to be there.

His mom led him from the house and into the car. He lent against the window and listened to the rain pelting it. He let the rain engulf him and keep his mind wandering until they reached the funeral home. He saw Sarah, Christian and Nic waiting just inside the doors; they were waiting for him. Once the car was parked, his mom came around and opened his door. He begrudgingly got out and made his way to the entrance. Sarah wrapped him in her arms despite the wetness of the rain. For the first time in his life he truly understood what it meant to draw strength from someone; without Sarah at his side, he knew that he would never make it through this day.

Hands joined tightly together he and Sarah walked into the viewing room. Mr. Tolliver greeted them and asked them to join him, Mrs. Tolliver, and Ryan in the front. It was odd leaving his mom, Christian, and Nic but Mr. Tolliver told them no one was closer to Ben than they were and it would make the family happy to have him and Sarah sit with them. For the briefest of moments, David felt an emotion other than sadness.

When the service started he was relieved that the Tollivers had opted for a non-traditional funeral. A brief prayer was said by a priest and then family and friends took turns sharing memories and stories about Ben. Sarah was asked to speak last and David was happy to know that she was able to get up and speak. She nervously approached the open coffin and then started to speak.

"I have been blessed to have known Ben since I was four years old. From the moment we first met in preschool we were inseparable. When we met David two years later our twosome became a trio. I knew that I had found the friends I would have for the rest of my life. We've shared some fantastic adventures over the years . . ." She stopped for a moment and wiped the tears from her eyes. She forced a smile to her face. "I'd like to share one of those with you today."

She pulled a folded, ragged looking piece of paper from her pocket. David knew what it was without a word as he had an exact duplicate of it in his wallet.

"Four years ago in freshman composition class we had been given the task of writing a essay on who we thought of as our hero. We could choose whomever we wanted but the catch was that we had to read them aloud to the whole class. We had about a week to prep and as we always did, Ben, David and I got together that first night to hash out our plans. We were so anxious to hear who the other was writing about. David was the first to share and said he had chosen his grandfather. I had gone back and forth between my parents or someone like Hillary Clinton. Ben however wouldn't tell us who he had chosen. He said we had to wait and see. We assumed he had chosen his Grandma Becker as he had been extremely close to her."

Sarah cleared her throat and cradled the paper to her chest for a moment as she tried to not burst into tears before she continued. David felt the same as he knew where the story was heading.

"On the day of presentations Ben asked if he could go first. He stood before our class and began to read. He hadn't chosen his grandma; he had chosen David and me. This is what he wrote."

Sarah unfolded the paper and started to read. David was transported back to ninth grade and the same emotions of surprise, pride and joy overtook him. He could see Ben standing before his class sharing such raw emotions and feelings for his best friends. He talked about how the three of them could always depend on the other for honesty, respect, love, laughter and support. In his deepest, darkest hours after his grandma died he discovered what true heroes he had in his life. When he let darkness envelope him, they provided the light he needed to see clearly. Ben shared so many feelings and thoughts beyond his years. He ended by saying he knew what true friendship was; it was the bond he shared with David and Sarah.

"Everyone was silent when Ben finished reading it to the class. David and I looked at each other and we both had tears in our eyes; even Mr. Shiner, our teacher, had tears in his eyes. I can't speak for David, but I know that I never felt so important or loved before." Sarah paused to wipe her eyes. "Naturally, no one in the class wanted to go after him because we all knew our compositions couldn't compare to his. Needless to say, but Ben received an A+ on it. That night, Ben handed David and I our own copies written in his own hand. I had a photocopy made of the original, which is framed in my room and this copy I have carried with me ever since. Ben is and will always be my hero. And . . ." She couldn't hold back the tears now. "I . . . (sob) will . . . miss . . . (sob) him . . . everyday."

Mrs. Tolliver placed a gentle hand on David's tightly clasped hands and did not remove it through the final prayer or as the incredibly packed room silently marched past Ben's casket; she let go once the final person was gone and the only remaining people in the room were the Tollivers and Sarah and David. Mrs. Tolliver hugged David and then hugged Sarah and thanked them for being with them.

Sarah and David approached the casket for their final goodbyes. Sarah went first. When she stepped back David slowly approached. He touched the cool lifeless hands that were coupled on Ben's unmoving chest; it was so hard to believe that these were the same hands that he had held, kissed, and longed to hold. Again, his eyes burned as more tears fell; he didn't wipe them away. This was the last time he could ever touch the person whom he loved more than anything.

David took off his ring and slid it into the breast pocket of Ben's suit. He bent forward and kissed Ben's cool forehead. With barely a whisper, David spoke. "I love you Ben. No one will ever replace you. I will always love you."

He backed away from the casket. Mr. and Mrs. Tolliver hugged him again. He whispered a thank you. David took Sarah's arm in his and they rejoined Christian, Nic and his mom for the drive to the cemetery.

The service at the grave was quick, since the rain still had not let up. Again, he and Sarah were asked to stand with the Tollivers and were able to toss the handful of earth on the casket as it was lowered into the ground. The wake was held in the banquet hall of Sarah's parent's hotel. David had been so amazed to see how many people had attended the funeral, so many friends and acquaintances. He was happy to see James, Stephanie, Chuck and Holly had also been able to come. James had come to the funeral parlor yesterday, but David hadn't seen him as he been completely withdrawn. As he entered the hall James was the first to come up and hug him. Sarah, Christian, Nic and him joined the group of friends as food was about to be served.

Stories of happy times were being shared, but David could not celebrate Ben's life with his friends. He was not able or ready to share the true feelings of his and Ben's relationship. As the occupants of his table rose to get food, he left the hall and sought out the room he and Ben had shared so many times in the Davidson's private wing.

He sat on the floor as he had done so many months ago when he and his mom had come here for refuge. He had thought his life was over then; he could almost laugh about it now. That had been so much easier than these past couple of days. He closed his eyes and tried to forget everything.

Someone knocked on the door some time later. He couldn't muster the strength to even answer. He waited a moment and the knocking continued as the door slowly opened. Nic stood in the hall with a tray of food in his hands.

"I thought you might be hungry."

David shrugged his shoulders. He had barely eaten in days and felt if he tried to eat something now he would throw up.

Nic entered the room and shut the door behind him. He placed the tray on a dresser and pulled a package from under his arms.

"Would it be okay if I sit with you for a little while?"

David nodded.

"Mr. and Mrs. Tolliver asked me to bring this up to you. They found it in Ben's luggage after the accident. They wanted to make sure you got it."

David accepted the package and noticed the simple tag with his name written so neatly in Ben's handwriting. He took a deep breath and slowly slid his finger between the silver paper exposing a leather bound book. His heart raced; at first he thought it was Ben's personal journal, but then he noticed this one had his and Ben's initials embossed on its cover.

He undid the leather strap and opened the cover. Ben's neat printing met his teary eyes.

David -

This collection of pictures, music lyrics, poems, clippings and personal writings that have inspired, encouraged and moved me over the years. I want to share them with you. I want to take you on journey through my thoughts, feelings, and desires that have made me the person I am today.

I have been so blessed to have you as a friend and now my boyfriend. For the first time in my life I know what love truly is. I look forward to the many journeys ahead of us.

I love you with all my heart.

Ben

David felt the tears begin to fall. He closed the book and clutched it close to his chest. This was too much for him to take; this journal was Ben.

Nic joined David on the floor and placed an arm around his shoulder. David rested his head on Nic's shoulder and let the rush of sorrow engulf him. He cried more than he had ever cried before.

* * * * *

David woke some time later, his head still resting on Nic's shoulder. Nic had his eyes closed but David knew he was not sleeping. He slowly lifted his head and saw Nic's eyes open and he smiled.

"Sorry about that."

"Don't apologize. I am sure you needed it."

"How long was I asleep?"

Nic pulled his arm from David's shoulder and rubbed it as he checked his watch.

"About an hour and a half."

"Oh . . . where's the journal?" He panicked as he realized he was no longer holding it.

"It's on the bed behind us. I moved it after you fell asleep so it wouldn't get damaged."

David sighed with relief. "Thank you." For a moment he had worried that he had dreamed receiving it.

"Most of the people have gone. Your mom left too, she knew you'd probably want to stay here tonight and be with Sarah."

He did want to stay, but he also wanted Christian and Nic here too. He tried not to sound so desperate but it came out far too rapidly as he asked Nic if he was staying too.

"Of course. I'll stay as long as you need me to."

A knock came from the door. Nic turned his head to look. David didn't say anything, he still wasn't sure if he was ready to see people. His conversation with Nic was the most he'd said to anyone in days. Nic looked at him with question. He reluctantly nodded his head in agreement.

"Come in." Nic announced.

James came into the room.

"Hey man, we're leaving, but I wanted to make sure I said goodbye and see if you were alright."

David nodded.

James knelt down before him and took David's hand and shook it, but did not release it.

"If you need anything from me just ask. Ben was a great guy and a good friend. I'm going to miss him a lot."

"Me too." David whispered.

"Can I share a quick story?"

Nervously, David nodded.

"Mr. T came over to our table sometime after you came upstairs and said that he didn't know how he was going to make it through today until he saw you kiss Ben's forehead. He said that simple gesture reaffirmed to him that Ben's life had been meaningful and blessed. He knew that Ben would never truly be gone."

David smiled weakly. Ben's life had been blessed, just as everyone who know him had been.

"It . . . was."

"I know, but . . ." James looked him straight in the eyes. "I know what Ben meant to you. I've known for a couple of weeks now."

David looked to Nic, who appeared to be as dumbfounded as he was. David looked back at James and saw a smile on his face.

"No one told me. I figured it out myself. I thought I might have imagined it at first, but it was so obvious at prom. I know I have the reputation of being a dumb jock, but I do have a brain."

"How . . . how . . . you're okay . . . ?"

"You are my friend and so was Ben. Nothing has changed here. I am truly, sorry for your loss, David. I mean that."

"Thank you."

James released his hand and stood up. "I meant what I said. If you need anything, I'm here. I'll stop by in a couple of days and check in on you. Take care."

James left as quickly as he arrived. Nic returned his arm around David who returned his head to Nic's shoulder. Though he heard encouraging words from James, he still couldn't process their entire meaning yet, it was going to be a long time before he could let himself be happy.

Sarah

Sarah and Ben had shared so much of their lives with each other; she felt as if she lost a part of herself. She wanted to scream and cry about the unfairness but at the same time she felt she had to be strong for David; she knew how much this was weighing on him as well. However, David had lost more than just a dear friend; he lost the love of his life. They were attempting to comfort each other and doing miserably; until tonight neither one could truly express their anguish to each other; both afraid to cause the other pain. Tonight, David had allowed her to read the journal Ben had left him.

David handed her the book and retreated to his new favorite place in the room, the window seat. Sarah took the book to a chair; she took a deep calming breath and slowly opened the cover. Turning the pages she was met with smiling photos of Ben, David and herself ranging from childhood to the present. She flipped through the book first looking at all the photos. So many memories were recalled; a true testament to their friendship. She returned to the beginning and began to read some of the entries. As she read she could easily hear Ben's deep voice reciting the text. She only read a couple of entries before she had to stop or she was going to become a sobbing mess.

She sat for a long time starting at the closed journal. It was something made with so much love and dedication. Again she felt the anger begin to rise; it was so unfair that Ben had been taken from them. Though Karen was being charged for her actions in the attack, it offered little comfort to the void she had caused in so many people's lives.

She felt David's hand on her shoulder, she rose and they embraced. They didn't need to say anything; they both knew what the other was feeling. She thanked him and left the room. She paused in the hall for a moment to catch her breath before she ventured down the stairs to join Christian in the kitchen. It had become their nightly meeting place before Christian would leave to go to his parent's house before they would meet again in the morning and begin their daily ritual of keeping David occupied.

In the two weeks since the wake, David had barely left his room. He would only leave it for meals, to visit Sarah in her room, or for their afternoon walk through the woods. He refused to attend his own graduation saying he wouldn't go without Ben. She, Nic, and Christian took turns spending time with David trying to get him to open up and talk. Nic seemed to be the only person able to get David to say more than a few words.

Christian met her at the kitchen door and she slumped into his arms and sighed. She wanted to cry but after reading Ben's words she felt so drained of energy she didn't think she could even must a tear.

"How did it go tonight, Sarah-bear?"

"Exhausting. He let me read some of the journal tonight. He said he reads it every night and thought I should read some of it too."

Christian nodded and smiled. They had been wondering if David had read any of it since the wake. Each time they entered the room it was always in the same spot. If someone mentioned it, David usually didn't respond.

"That is a good sign; at least he isn't ignoring it like we thought. It is going to be slow, but he is making progress."

"Yeah." Sarah whispered.

Christian hugged her again and led her to the table where their nightly snack of Oreo cookies and milk awaited them. Sarah sat heavily in the chair and picked up her cookie but didn't eat it.

"What is it?"

She offered a smile and tried to hide her pain, but she couldn't hold it for long. Christian's hands touched hers.

"I . . . it was if he was standing next to me. As . . . as I read his words, oh Christian, it was . . . overwhelming. It was Ben's . . . it was Ben's words . . . they . . ."

She couldn't finish her thoughts; she was torn between her feelings. Reading Ben's words filled her with love and peace, knowing he was still with them, but at the same time she felt so incredibly lonely and sad. She heard him in her mind and that gave her hope but she questioned how long she would be able to remember what his voice sounded like.

"I miss him so much."

"I miss him too, Sarah-bear. Ben will always be with us. He will never be forgotten."

"I . . . I know that. It just doesn't help right now though."

Nicholas

Nic flipped through the journal with a sense of deep sadness but also a longing. He could see the bonds of friendship, compassion, and love shared between David, Sarah and Ben so clearly. Even the most innocent of pictures clearly expressed the bond of friendship. He could see the smiles, the laughter, and joy these three friends shared. He found himself wishing he could have become a part of their inner sanctum earlier than he had.

He felt so honored when David first suggested he read the journal, yet he passed on the honor. He felt that it was something unique and special that only David and Sarah should have the privilege to see. However the more time he and David spent together the more he realized that David felt it was important for Nic to know more about Ben. It was a conversation with Christian that finally convinced him to accept David's offer.

He and Christian were having lunch and the conversation turned to the journal. Nic shared David's invitation and Christian asked him why he felt reluctant to accept it. When Nic shared his thoughts, Christian asked him why he felt that he wasn't one of the privileged. Nic tried to say that the history of the trio was one that was so rich and personal that he felt it would be an intrusion. Christian reminded him how Ben had sought him out on many occasions to ask questions but mainly to simply talk. He went on to say that in the short time Nic had known Ben he had been included in many of the group's conversations and decisions. Christian then shared that in the weeks since Ben's death, Nic had done more for David and Sarah than any other friend. He then said that David would not have offered if he didn't feel Ben would have approved of Nic reading it.

So when David offered again tonight, he stumbled over his answer but could see a glimmer of a smile on David's face when he said yes. He was so nervous when David handed him the journal, he felt as if he was holding the most precious of treasures. He wiped his hands on his jeans afraid to leave any mark on the pages.

He gently closed the journal and closed his eyes; it had been such a moving journey to see the lives of his friends before and after he joined them. He had a greater understanding of Ben, Sarah and David. He couldn't express the raw emotions he felt, nothing he had known before could come close.

He opened his eyes; David was watching him intently.

"Thank you, David. I feel . . . honored and proud. I know that doesn't make much sense, but I don't know if I can say more at the moment."

"I understand."

He handed the journal to David who held it close to his chest for a minute and then carefully laid it on the table next to the bed.

"Nic, can I . . . can I ask you . . . something?"

"Always."

"Remember the night of prom? We were in the suite and Ben and I were talking about our future?"

"Yes."

"I'm, I'm thinking I need to do that."

Nic wasn't exactly sure what David was getting at. That night he and Ben had said so many things about traveling and going to California for school. Was David telling him he was leaving?

"What do you mean?"

"I think I need to go." David looked around the room. "Every where I look, I see Ben."

"Of course, you have so many memories here."

"We also had dreams about where we were going. I feel it's important for me to try to fulfill some of those. I've got some money and I need to try."

Nic understood where David was coming from. He was struggling to move forward but felt it important to honor the dreams he and Ben had created.

"I think Ben would like that. Do, do you know where you want to go?"

"I think so, but . . . I . . . I have something else to say, well, actually there is something . . . I'd like to ask you."

"Sure thing."

"Would you . . . would you be interested in coming with me?"

"What?"

"It's just, you have been such a good friend to me these past couple of months, but especially since Ben . . . since . . ." He couldn't finish.

"David, I am so honored that you would ask me, but do you think I am the right person. What about Sarah? The two of you need each other so much right now."

"I . . . know. But . . . but I think I need something . . . Sarah will always be my closest friend, don't get me wrong, but she and Christian have their plans and I can't ask her to change them. I know she may not completely understand, but I need to make a fresh start. I'm not breaking my ties with her or anything, but I . . ."

"You don't need to justify anything. I think I understand what you are saying."

Nic rose from his chair and paced back and forth. He had been caught off guard by David's suggestion. He cared for the young man so much and wanted to be there for him in any way he could but at the same time he wondered if he could truly just pack up and leave. He had ties here, but maybe it was time to try something new as well. He'd just graduated and didn't have a job lined up so there was no problem there. What was holding him here then?

It was then he remembered again how proud he had been to be included in the lives of Ben and David. He had been so happy when they began emailing, texting and calling. Immediately he relished his role as gay big brother to them. David was part of his family now and he wanted to be there for him.

"If you need to think . . ."

"No, I don't need to think about it." Nic announced. "David, I would be honored to come with you."

Sarah

The door to David's suite was open and Sarah could see his luggage was packed and lined up by the dresser waiting to be taken down to his car. She scanned the room; it was spotless. No crumpled blankets on the floor, no shirts casually thrown on the chair, and no boots lying haphazardly next to the bed. It was if he was already gone. Though she knew that he was going to leave at some point, she had grown so accustomed to having him here everyday. It had made the last few weeks so much easier.

She inched her way into the room knowing that David was in his usual spot, the window seat. He had his back to her as usual, but instead of blankly staring out at the grounds he was staring at the newly acquired tattoo of Ben's name on his wrist. His fingers longingly circled the tattoo as she heard him whisper Ben's name. She was about to say something when his fingers left his wrist and picked up something that had been lying next to him. She knew what it was; she recognized the black wood frame instantly since she had a matching one in her own room. The frames held a matted black and white photo of Sarah, Christian, David and Ben during their dinner with Nic. Christian had given them to the gang as presents on prom. Until last week it had just been another photo of the group, but now it was part of the last photos taken of Ben alive.

"He looks so happy."

"He was." She stammered. She didn't realize that David knew she was in the room. "We were all happy that night."

"I haven't been able to look at it until now." David's fingers now traced Ben's image over and over through the glass.

"When I first noticed that mom had included it with the stuff she sent over I buried it in the dresser, but last night Nic dug it out and told me I had to look at it. He said I couldn't ignore it anymore."

Sarah's hand gently caressed his head and then rested on his shoulder. "He was right." She could feel David's steady breathing.

"It's so hard. I see . . . I see his smiling face and I keep expecting him to come in here and tell me it was all a bad dream. Every where I look I see him."

David pulled away from her touch and left the window seat. He walked over to his luggage and carefully placed the frame inside one of his smaller bags. He wiped his eyes, sniffled and attempted to smile but his lips only quivered and the tears began rolling down his face.

"I'm sorry. I told myself . . . (sob) . . . I wasn't going to cry."

Sarah wiped at her own tearing eyes.

"It's okay. I miss him too."

"Are you . . . is it okay that I am leaving?"

"David, you have to do what is right for you."

"I can't stay here anymore . . . its too hard."

"You do not have to explain."

When Nic first told them that David was talking about wanting to use the money his grandparents had left him to get out of town and travel because he needed to go somewhere he wasn't constantly reminded of Ben, Sarah had to admit she knew exactly what David meant. They had grown up in this town and they had so many memories, it was a constant reminder to David.

"Have you decided where you are going yet?"

"Yeah, I was thinking that maybe we would go to California. Ben and I were planning on going there so he could go to school."

"You both wanted to go there so badly." Sarah said happily. "I'm glad too that Nic agreed to go with you."

"Yeah, I would have asked you, but . . ."

"I told you before; you don't need to explain, David." Sarah said interrupting him. She knew the old Sarah would have become jealous and fear she was being cast aside. However, she had grown up a great deal in the past few weeks; she knew David needed something different now. She and David would always be close, but he was going through something she couldn't help him with and he needed a different kind of support now. She understood that and would give him all the love and understanding she could.

She hugged him and kissed his cheek.

"I'm not running away. We'll call, text and email just as much as before."

"I know that. I've already made sure Nic is to see that you do; because if you don't, I'll be on the first plane to kick you in the butt."

"I would expect nothing less from my oldest, dearest, and most treasured friend."

"Promise me something, David?"

"What?"

"Don't shut yourself off from love. Ben would want you to keep living and loving."

"I . . . I don't know if I can promise that, exactly. What if . . . what if I promise to try?"

"That is perfect."

Made in the USA
Las Vegas, NV
03 February 2025

17419715R00152